"Tell me one good reason why you and I can't continue to be lovers."

Fury ignited along her veins. *Sex!* Was that all he ever wanted from her? Was that all he ever wanted from any woman whom he didn't rate as a perfect ten?

"Very well," she bit out. "I'll give you one very good reason. Soon, you won't want me as your lover. Soon, that wonderful chemistry you spoke of will fail to spark, because I'll be too big and fat to inspire much in you except revulsion. Yes, Lewis, I see the penny's beginning to drop. Yes, that's right. I'm going to have a baby!"

Relax and enjoy our fabulous series about spirited women and gorgeous men, whose passion results in pregnancies...sometimes unexpected! Of course, the birth of a baby is always a joyful event, and we can guarantee that our characters will become besotted moms and dads—but what happened in those nine months before?

Share the surprises, emotions, dramas and suspense as our parents-to-be come to terms with the prospect of bringing a new little life into the world.... All will discover that the business of making babies brings with it the most special love of all...

Look out next month for our final arrival—
a Christmas baby—in
The Yuletide Child (#2070)
by Charlotte Lamb

MIRANDA LEE

The Boss's Baby

EXPECTING

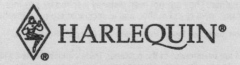

HARLEQUIN®

TORONTO • NEW YORK • LONDON
AMSTERDAM • PARIS • SYDNEY • HAMBURG
STOCKHOLM • ATHENS • TOKYO • MILAN • MADRID
PRAGUE • WARSAW • BUDAPEST • AUCKLAND

ISBN 0-373-12064-8

THE BOSS'S BABY

First North American Publication 1999.

Copyright © 1998 by Miranda Lee.

This edition published by arrangement with Harlequin Books S.A.

Visit us at www.romance.net

Printed in U.S.A.

CHAPTER ONE

'IS THERE anything wrong, Olivia?'

Olivia glanced up to find her boss frowning down at her from his considerable height. With great difficulty, she pushed aside her whirling thoughts and smiled one of those small plastic smiles she used round the office.

'Not at all,' she said, but the smile felt like cement. 'Everything's fine. I'm fine.' Dropping her eyes from his probing gaze, Olivia busied herself, mindlessly tidying her desk top. She wasn't about to confide her personal problems to her boss. They didn't have that kind of relationship.

When she'd been hired eighteen months before, Lewis had warned her that his wife had not been happy with his previous secretary's far too familiar manner, and far too glamorous mode of dressing.

Olivia had been only too happy to present the reserved and conservative image which found favour with the boss's wife. She was a reserved type of girl anyway, and had always been a conservative dresser. Years before she'd settled on always wearing basic black to work, with the odd white or cream blouse thrown in. That way, the only accessories she needed were black.

Her wardrobe was very economical, as was the simple hairstyle which saw her long straight dark auburn hair swept back from her face and secured in a big loop at the nape of her neck, the anchoring band always covered by a plain black clip or bow. Economical too was the minimal amount of make-up and jewellery which adorned the rest of her.

On her rare visits to the office, the boss's wife had never had any reason to be suspicious or jealous of her husband's new private secretary. Olivia made sure she never crossed the line where Lewis was concerned. She had no reason to. Tall, dark and handsome her boss might be, but she was very much in love with the man she was going to marry.

Ironically, Lewis and his wife had still broken up six months back, an event which had propelled the boss into a permanently morose and introverted mood. His noticing Olivia's own wretched and distracted state of mind was unusual to say the least, and quite irritating. Why couldn't he have stayed buried in his laboratory all morning, as had become his habit lately? Why did he have to come out and pry into her own private misery?

'You don't look fine,' he persisted.

'Oh?' Her hands automatically lifted to check her hair.

'I'm not talking about how you *look*,' Lewis snapped, 'but how you're acting. Ever since you got in this morning you've been just sitting there, staring into space.'

Space. Now that was a word Olivia wasn't too thrilled with this morning. Space! Nicholas, her fiancé, had told her last night that he needed more *space.* It was one of his excuses for opting out of their relationship. That and about a million others!

'You haven't even turned on your computer,' Lewis added, as though that were the crime of the century.

A glance up at the wall clock showed Olivia it *was* almost nine-thirty. She'd been sitting at her desk doing nothing for over an hour. Wearily, she reached forward to snap on the screen, muttering, 'Sorry,' as she did so.

Lewis's sigh was full of male frustration. 'For pity's sake, Olivia, you don't have to apologise! I don't give a damn whether you work or not. I'm *concerned* about you; can't you see that?'

'Concerned?' she repeated disbelievingly as her eyes lifted back to his.

It had been a long time since anyone had expressed concern about her, possibly because she always portrayed such a coolly efficient image. Her parents always thought she had it all together, as did her two younger sisters. It was *she* who usually handed out the advice, happily lecturing her family on matters of budgeting and goal-setting.

She'd had her life totally mapped out...till last night, when Nicholas had packed his bags and stormed out of their flat, leaving her alone with the person he'd nastily described at length during the previous sixty minutes, that controlling, stingy, boring bitch who'd been ruining his life for the past two years, ruling her every waking moment, smothering his personality and turning him into a spineless, mindless wimp.

He was tired of saving money, tired of eating in and very tired of only having sex in a bed!

He was younger than she was, he'd reminded her scathingly. He wanted some fun before he settled down. Some fun and some *space*. He didn't want to get married just yet. He didn't want the responsibility of a mortgage and kids. He certainly didn't want to buy a family car. He wanted to drive a Porsche. He wanted to travel. He wanted other women, women who knew that oral was not just a brand of toothbrush!

His dumping on their sex life really stung, because she'd never imagined their love life had been inadequate, or that Nicholas was so discontent in that area. For one thing, he'd always told her he fully understood her distaste for certain forms of foreplay. In fact, he'd claimed to share her feelings on the matter.

'There's not a spontaneous sexual bone in your body, Olivia,' he'd flung at her in parting. 'You have no idea how to make a man happy. No bloody idea!'

At the time she'd thought he was mad. Now, suddenly, crushingly, she believed him.

'Olivia? What *is* it?' her boss demanded to know.

Valiantly, she fought back the tears.

'Is it Nicholas?'

All she could do was nod, her eyes dropping lest she lose the battle.

'Is he ill?'

She shook her head from side to side.

'Don't tell me you two have split up!'

Olivia winced at the note of disbelief in his voice. Twenty-four hours ago she would have been just as sceptical over such a thing happening. She'd been so sure they were right for each other; that they'd wanted the same things. Marriage next year. A house the year after that, then their first baby before she turned thirty.

Now, the only thing Olivia could see for herself by thirty was loneliness. It had taken her years of looking to find Nicholas. She was already twenty-seven...

'Please, Lewis,' she said, stiffening her shoulders and her quavering bottom lip while she brought up the correspondence file on the computer. 'I don't want to talk about it.'

She felt his eyes hard upon her, but simply refused to meet them. She stared straight ahead at the screen and began tapping on the keyboard.

'Don't worry too much, Olivia,' Lewis said. 'Give him a day or two and he'll come to his senses. I'll bet he comes crawling back before the week is out.'

Olivia's head jerked up, hope flooding her heart.

'Do you think so?'

'No sane man would leave a girl like you, Olivia,' her boss pronounced firmly. 'Trust me.'

Nicholas *did* come back the following weekend, but he wasn't crawling, and he didn't stay. He merely collected a few personal things he'd left behind—some toiletries and his CD collection. As he strode out the door with hurtful nonchalance, he sarcastically told Olivia she could keep the wonderful furniture they'd been sharing.

From her front window, she watched him drive off in a brand-new black Porsche on which he must have wasted his entire savings, money which was to have been half of the deposit on the perfectly planned home they'd been going to build together, and in which they'd been going to rear their two perfectly planned children.

Olivia was left to weep over the thrift-shop bargains which she'd bought for a song then painstakingly stripped back and painted, thinking she was saving money for their future together. She wept on and off for another week, her depression increased by the closeness of Christmas. People were supposed to be happy at Christmas!

Olivia functioned at work on automatic pilot but wasn't able to force herself to do much at home, even eat. Lunchtimes were spent wandering aimlessly through Parramatta Mall. She told Lewis she had Christmas shopping to do, but in fact just wanted to get away from his gently probing eyes. Her boss in sympathetic mode was not one she was used to, or comfortable with.

It was testimony to Olivia's distracted state that her last day at work for the year was suddenly upon her and she hadn't even bought Lewis a Christmas card, let alone a gift. Guilt consumed her as she picked up the lovely gold-embossed card Lewis had given her, not to mention the huge box of chocolates, which she'd slipped into her bottom drawer for low blood sugar emergencies.

She would have to slip out later and buy him something. She doubted she'd be missed. The entire staff of Altman Industries would be busy celebrating the annual five-week shutdown with a Christmas party to end all company Christmas parties. There would be a marquee set up on the lawn, dancing on the factory floor, food to tempt even the most stringent dieter, beer by the keg and cases of first-class champagne.

It would cost Lewis a fortune, Olivia knew.

But it was a tradition, and he could afford it. Altman Industries might be a relatively small company, but its profits rose every year, even more so after they'd gone international three years ago.

Lewis had started the company in a backyard garage over a decade back. An industrial chemist by training but a naturalist by inclination, he'd combined science and nature to produce a simple range of skin care products for men, starting with a shaving cream and a combination aftershave-lotion-cum moisturiser. A soap swiftly followed, then a shower gel, shampoo and conditioner. Three years back, a hugely successful cologne had been added to the range.

Lewis had been smart enough to employ a good advertising agency from the beginning and they'd come up with the catchy brand name of All Man, a derivation of Lewis's surname of Altman. Using famous Australian sportsmen to endorse the products had brought instant success.

Lewis had swiftly moved from the limiting garage into a modern factory and office complex site in the centrally located industrial park at Ermington. Expansion had initially meant a huge overdraft at the bank, but it wasn't long before Altman Industries were back in the black and posting profits that were the envy of its larger competitors.

Next year, Lewis planned to expand production to include an All Woman line. He'd already created the basic skin and hair care range and was now working on the perfume.

Olivia didn't know all these facts from private conversations with Lewis, although she naturally gleaned some of the information in her position as private secretary to the owner of the company. She'd read a recent article written about him in *Good Business* magazine which had done a series on successful Sydney companies, and their owners.

She'd also learned that Lewis was thirty-four years old, an only child whose father had died when he was five. He'd been well educated due to his mother's working up to three jobs, for which he was eternally grateful. There'd been an accompanying photograph of an elegant grey-haired lady who looked around sixty. One of the reasons for his focused ambition had been a desire to repay his mother for all the sacrifices she'd made for him. He wanted to give her everything she'd never had.

Olivia had never actually met Lewis's mother, but had spoken to her often on the phone. Mrs Altman senior didn't live with her son, even now that he'd separated from his wife. She had her own address in Drummoyne, an inner-city suburb which hugged the harbour.

Olivia had always sensed that Mrs Altman hadn't liked her son's choice of wife. Given the closeness of their relationship, maybe Lewis's mother would not have liked *any* woman Lewis married. The article had only briefly mentioned Lewis's marriage of two years, saying his estranged wife was 'in fashion' and their separation was amicable.

Olivia had laughed over that at the time. Amicable, my foot!

She didn't feel like laughing this Friday morning. Only now could she fully understand Lewis's devastation when Dinah left him. Olivia had never felt so low in her whole life. The thought of attending the Christmas party was unpalatable. How could she possibly enjoy herself? All that eating and drinking, not to mention dancing. The only dancing Olivia cared for was the old-fashioned kind.

If last year's Christmas party was anything to go by, that was not the kind of dancing with which the factory floor would resonate. Discoing would be the order of the day. Olivia didn't like gyrating around virtually on her own. She wasn't uninhibited enough to enjoy making a public exhibition of herself.

She wasn't uninhibited enough to make a *private* exhibition of herself, either. Nicholas's parting barb about being bored with always having sex in a bed had been haunting her. Because he was so right. She'd never made love with him anywhere else but in bed. She'd never even made love on *top* of the bed!

Being on top in any shape or form was not in her limited résumé of sexual experiences. Neither were any of the other more exotic foreplays and positions. When she'd met Nicholas at twenty-five, she'd still been a virgin. Nicholas was too, surprisingly, although he *had* only been twenty-two at the time. They'd muddled along together and sex hadn't been a great success for a while. But they'd finally mastered the basics, and she'd honestly thought Nicholas was happy in bed. She'd never refused him and he'd always come, even when she hadn't. It seemed now she'd overestimated his pleasure and satisfaction in her body, not to mention her less than adventurous technique.

The telephone ringing snapped her out of her broodingly introspective mood for a moment.

'Mr Altman's office,' came her automatic response. 'Olivia Johnson speaking. May I help you?'

'You certainly may, my dear. I'd like to speak to that son of mine, if he's not too busy. I realise it's party day.'

'He's still in his laboratory, Mrs Altman. I'll put you through.'

'Before you do, my dear, I just wanted to wish you a happy Christmas and to thank you for always being so nice to me on the phone.'

'Why, thank you, Mrs Altman. And a happy Christmas to you too.'

'What are you doing for Christmas?'

'I'm going home to my parents' place.'

'And where's that?'

'They live near Morisset.'

'Morisset? That's up on the central coast, isn't it?'

'Yes, between Gosford and Newcastle. It's about a two-hour train trip from Sydney. Less from Hornsby where I catch it.'

'I see. Well, we'll have to go to lunch together one day next year, dear. I'd love to put a face and figure to the voice. I asked Lewis once what you looked like and all he said was you were a brunette with intelligent brown eyes. When I asked what kind of figure you had, he looked perplexed for a moment, and then said, "Sort of medium."'

Although piqued, Olivia couldn't really blame Lewis. The tailored black suits she favoured in the office were not designed to stand out, or display her body. Her skirts were never too short or too tight. Any deep Vs in her jackets were always filled in with a simple top or shirt-style blouse. Today's outfit was no exception. If she'd remembered the Christmas party Olivia might have worn something a little brighter. But she hadn't and that was that!

'You know, I haven't been into the office since that other awful girl was ensconced behind your desk,' Mrs Altman senior was saying. 'The last time I visited, she was wearing a dress cut down to her navel. Not to mention very little underwear. As for perfume... I think she must have bathed in it. Poor Lewis. I finally understood why his ex-wife used to complain he smelt like the cosmetics counter in David Jones every time he came home at night.'

Olivia didn't go perfumeless. But the small spray of Eternity she allowed herself every morning was very discreet.

'Unfortunately, it's very difficult to get rid of employees these days,' the boss's mother rattled on. 'If Lewis had sacked the infernal girl, he'd have found himself in court before he knew it, trying to explain to a judge why he'd fired this suddenly prim and proper creature dressed in pin-tucks and a Peter Pan collar.'

Olivia felt the corners of her mouth crinkling with

amusement. 'I gathered Lewis *was* very relieved when she left to go overseas.'

'More than relieved, I can tell you. But he's been very happy with you, dear. You haven't given him a moment's worry or trouble!'

Olivia wasn't sure if she liked the sound of that, or not.

'Although he *did* express some concern the other night about your having had a lovers' tiff with your boyfriend. He said you were very down in the mouth about it.'

'Yes, well...' Her voice trailed off. She really didn't want to discuss Nicholas with Mrs Altman any more than Lewis.

'Don't let pride get in your way, dear,' came the unwanted advice. 'Call him. Say you're sorry, even if it *was* his fault. After all, what's a bit of grovelling when all's said and done?'

Olivia's eyebrows shot up. She'd never grovelled to anyone in her life and she wasn't about to start now. Still... Mrs Altman did have a point. Pride did sometimes get in the way of reconciliations. She reasoned there was a huge difference between grovelling and giving Nicholas a call. She could use the excuse of wishing him a happy Christmas. He would be in his office right now. She could be talking to him in seconds. Her heart raced as hope reformed.

As soon as Olivia put Mrs Altman through to Lewis she dialled before she could think better of it. Nicholas's telephone rang several times before being picked up.

'Nickie's desk,' breathed a female voice.

Olivia was taken aback. 'Renee?' she asked hesi-
tantly. 'Is that you?' Renee was a colleague of
Nicholas who sometimes answered his phone when
he was away from his desk.

'Renee resigned some time back,' came the husky
reply. 'I'm Yvette. Her replacement.'

Renee's replacement. Named Yvette. And she
called Nicholas Nickie.

Olivia began to feel sick. 'Could I speak to
Nicholas, please?'

There was a small silence on the other end of the
phone, then a melodramatic sigh. 'Is that Olivia, by
any chance?'

'Put Nicholas on, please.'

'I can't. He's not here. He's gone to the little men's
room. You're wasting your time, anyway. He doesn't
want to see or talk to you ever again. He has me now
and I'm all he wants.'

Olivia sucked in a shaky breath. With a great effort
of will, she kept her voice quite calm. 'And just how
long have you been everything Nicholas wants?'

'Longer than you think. Face it, honey,' Yvette
purred down the line. 'You haven't got what it takes
to keep a man. It's not a female's organisational and
management abilities which win the day. Nickie could
get that from a computer. Or a cleaner. What he wants
is passion. And spontaneity. And fun.'

'Sex, you mean,' Olivia shot back, knowing now
where Nicholas had got most of his verbal armoury
during their final argument.

'Same thing.'

'You think he didn't get sex from me?' she threw

at this heartless creature who thought nothing of taking someone else's man.

'Not the kind he wanted, honey. Gotta go. We're all off down the pub for Chrissie drinks. Bye bye. Oh, and happy Christmas!'

Olivia was left listening to a dead line.

Suddenly, a rage began to simmer deep within her, a dark rebellious rage. Slamming the phone down, she jumped up from behind her desk, hot blood racing through her veins.

Going for Chrissie drinks, were they? Well, good for them. But she was going one better. She was going to a Chrissie party and by God she was going to party. She was going to party all day and she was going to forget. Forget Nicholas and Yvette. Forget that her future had been cruelly smashed. Forget everything but having fun!

Olivia stripped off her jacket and dropped it over the back of her chair. Having fun shouldn't be too hard. Not once she got a few glasses of champagne into her.

She was a happy drunk. Or she thought she would be. She'd never actually been drunk before. But a couple of glasses of wine always made her feel good.

And, dear God, she needed to feel good. She needed to feel good very, very badly!

Tugging the anchoring bow from the nape of her neck, she shook her head till her hair spilled halfway down her back. Flicking open the top two buttons of her blouse, she gave another defiant toss of her head, then marched determinedly in the direction of the music.

CHAPTER TWO

By two that afternoon, Olivia felt more than good. She felt fantastic. If she'd known champagne was such a great antidepressant she'd have tried it earlier. From her third glass, everything had begun to improve. Her mood. The music. The men.

By the time she'd consumed her first bottle of bubbly, one of the sales reps, a thirtyish womaniser named Phil, whom she wouldn't normally have given the time of day, started to seem genuinely charming. He'd been chatting away to her for over half an hour when Olivia first became aware of Lewis frowning at her. He was standing with a group from marketing near one of the trestles laden with food, a glass of beer in one hand and a slice of Christmas cake in the other.

Her boss's near scowl evoked a dark defiance in Olivia. Lewis wasn't her keeper. She had every right to have some harmless fun if she wanted to. Anyone would think she was doing something wrong instead of what every other single, unattached female here was doing: flirting and having a generally good time!

When Phil asked her to dance, Olivia didn't hesitate. Putting down her near empty glass and placing her hand in his outstretched fingers, she allowed him to draw her into the centre of the factory floor. The music switched from a softer number to a heady, throbbing beat which stirred her blood, and her general feeling of rebellion, ensuring that she smiled at Phil a little more widely, and danced a lot more provocatively.

Olivia discovered a primitive sense of rhythm she hadn't known she had, her body taking on a life of its own, undulating with all the grace and sensuality of a belly dancer, her arms reaching up above her head like two cobras under the hypnotic influence of a snake charmer's music.

The realisation that Lewis's narrowed blue gaze was riveted to her suddenly sinuous body did not go unnoticed by Olivia. Instantly, she became very conscious of her femininity: the way her full breasts were swaying beneath her blouse; the sensual swing of her womanly hips; the heat being generated in her secret places. It was a most exhilarating and arousing experience.

Olivia felt so sexy, it was sinful! She could have danced for ever, displaying herself shamelessly in front of the men's gawking eyes.

But especially one man's.

Shocking her boss out of his complacent attitude towards her was giving her a real buzz. It felt good to have him look at her for once as a woman capable of attracting men, maybe even capable of attracting *him*.

Actually, it felt more than good. It felt…thrilling.

The music, however, came to an end, and the disc jockey announced he was having a break.

'I had no idea,' Phil murmured as he guided her from the factory floor, 'that you could be like this.'

Picking up a frosted glass of champagne from a nearby table, he pressed it into her hot little hands.

'Like what?' she asked in a breathy voice to rival Yvette's.

Phil's leering smile sent warning bells ringing faintly in her fuzzy brain. The realisation of where Phil thought their flirtation was heading brought a momentary jab of conscience, but she easily brushed it aside. That was another thing about being deliciously drunk, she realised. You didn't fret over things. So Phil was going to be disappointed at the end of the day. So what? No real harm done.

Sipping her drink, she glanced idly around to see if Lewis was still watching her.

He wasn't. In fact, he was nowhere in sight.

Perversely, Olivia felt quite put out.

'Another dance?' Phil suggested.

Olivia was startled to find that the prospect of dancing without Lewis watching her held no appeal at all. In fact, all of a sudden, she'd lost interest in staying where she was.

'Sorry,' she said abruptly, 'but there's something else I have to do right now.'

Leaving Phil gaping after her, she strode across the factory floor to where the champagne was chilling in a huge vat. Extracting an opened bottle from its bed of ice, Olivia collected two clean glasses and set off in the direction of the main office block.

She found Lewis not in his laboratory, but in his office. He was standing at the window which had a view of the rolling front lawns, but not much else. His grey suit jacket had been discarded along with his tie, both thrown carelessly across the black leather chesterfield standing between them. Staring through the window, he absently undid his cuffs and began rolling up the sleeves of his crisp white shirt.

Without making her presence known, Olivia stood in the open doorway and just stared at him.

He was an exceptionally good-looking man, she finally conceded. A fact she'd always known but which she hadn't faced before with such honesty. That was another fringe benefit of being tipsy. Smiling ruefully to herself, Olivia decided to call it alcoholic enlightenment.

'So there you are!' she exclaimed gaily, and launched herself towards his desk, kicking the door shut behind her.

He whirled, then frowned at her. 'What in hell do you think you're doing?' he said when she set the glasses up on his desk and slopped in some champagne, spilling a little on the black lacquered top.

'Bringing the party to you, boss.' She threw him a saucy smile as she weaved her way over to him, thankful that the glasses were only half full. 'This is the one day in the year when we don't work around here. And that includes you. If you think you're going to hide yourself away in that infernal laboratory today, then you can think again. Here. Take this!' Having deposited one glass into his reluctant grip, she clinked her glass to his then lifted it to her lips, her eyes dancing at him over the rim. 'Merry Christmas, Lewis.'

'Olivia,' he said drily, making no attempt to drink. 'You're not just merry, you're sozzled.'

She laughed. 'I am, aren't I?'

'You're going to have one hell of a hangover in the morning,' he warned.

'I'll worry about that in the morning. Meanwhile, I'm having fun.'

One of his dark eyebrows lifted in a sardonic arch. 'So I noticed. You haven't forgotten Phil Baldwin's reputation with women, have you?'

'No.'

'For pity's sake, Olivia, if you must have revenge on Nicholas then pick yourself someone with a little more discretion. I really don't want the likes of Phil going round boasting that he had sex with my secretary at the Christmas party, all right?'

'You think I'd let him do that?'

'I don't know what to think.' His eyes carried a strange confusion as they roved over her, taking in her wild tumble of hair before dropping down to the shadowed cleavage between her breasts. 'When you let your hair down, Olivia,' he muttered tautly, 'you really let your hair down.'

The air was suddenly thick between them. Thick and hot and electric. The storm which had been brewing in Olivia all day gathered intensity. Lightning licked along her veins. Thunder roared in her temples. Her heart began to pound. Her eyes flashed and glittered.

'At least you noticed I was a woman,' she said huskily.

'Hard not to.'

'Would *you* like to have sex with me, Lewis?'

He was shocked, she could see. Yet along with the

shock lay a decided fascination. He couldn't take his eyes off her. She took advantage of his momentary stillness to close the distance between them and press herself against him, oh, so lightly. His nostrils flared with more shock.

Olivia was beyond shock; beyond everything but having Lewis look at her as he had out on the factory floor. A blistering desire was inflaming her senses while obliterating her conscience. All she could think of was having her boss admit he wanted her, having him powerless to resist her incredible expertise.

Boring, Nicholas had called her. If only he could see her now. Lewis wasn't looking at her as though she were boring.

Reaching up on tiptoe, Olivia brushed her lips tantalisingly against his.

He froze. But only for a second or two. When she kissed him a second time, more firmly this time, his lips softened against hers, parting as hers parted. When her tongue-tip darted forward to flick over his, he gave a low moan of sexual surrender.

A dark triumph filled her soul. Smiling, she drew back to survey his flushed face and startled mouth with a wicked satisfaction. 'I'll just be a moment,' she murmured.

She sipped her drink all the way to the door, finishing it by the time she reached to snap on the deadlock. Turning, she arched a naughty eyebrow at him. 'We don't want to be disturbed, do we?'

Somewhere, in the furthest reaches of her mind, she knew she was being outrageous. But nothing was going to stop her. Any qualms were ruthlessly buried underneath the roller-coaster excitement of the moment.

His eyes never left hers during her slow return across the room. They glittered and flashed, telling her of his own excitement.

She deposited her glass on the desk on the way, but made no attempt to relieve him of his, taking his free hand in hers and drawing him round to the roomy leather chesterfield.

He sat down in the middle where she directed, hot blue eyes burning into her while she kicked off her shoes and curled herself up next to him.

'Now,' she breathed, and took the untouched drink from his hand, 'we'll finish this up together, shall we?'

When she pressed the glass to his lips, he drank obediently, saying nothing when it was her turn. Determined not to be unnerved by his silence, she drained the glass, then dropped it over the back of the chesterfield onto the plush carpet. Cupping his face, she kissed him, at first lightly, then more deeply, making him moan.

With surprisingly nimble fingers, she managed to undo his shirt as she kissed him, pushing back the sides and smoothing her hands seductively over his bared chest.

He felt marvellous. Firm and muscular, with just enough body hair to exude a masculinity which was decidedly arousing. Lewis had a great body, she decided, probably because he balanced his sometimes sedentary lifestyle with rigorous workouts in the gym.

Olivia's primary goal of seducing *him* began to blur

as her own desires kicked in. Her head spun and she dragged her mouth from his to lick and kiss where her hands had been. When she grazed over a nipple, he sucked in sharply, tellingly. With a teasing wickedness she hadn't known she possessed, she deliberately avoided his nipples after that till they grew erect on their own, only then doing what he obviously craved.

'Oh, God,' he groaned aloud when she tugged on one of the tight little buds with her teeth.

The naked passion of his outburst thrilled her, making her torment him further till his chest was rising and falling with a raw ragged panting. When her kisses travelled down towards his navel and her hands found the zip on his trousers, his hands clamped down shakily over hers.

'No,' he protested. But unconvincingly, she thought.

Smiling seductively, she took his hands and stretched them up and out, spreading them wide on the back of the chesterfield. Her own body had to practically lie on top of his to do so, her breasts squashing against the hard expanse of his chest. The feel of his impressive erection pressing into the softness of her stomach was both reassuring and arousing. Somehow, she didn't think Lewis would object for long to what she had in mind.

And she had a lot of things in mind. All those things Nicholas thought her incapable of. All those things darling little Yvette had been giving *her* boyfriend in *his* office.

The need for revenge blended with her own need,

bringing a reckless mix which sent fire licking along her veins and a ruthless determination into her heart.

'Shh,' she murmured as she licked Lewis's parched lips. 'You want me to. You know you do.'

His strangled swear word only made her smile. 'Yes. Soon,' she promised. 'But first just lie back and enjoy. We don't want to rush things now, do we?'

Olivia smiled again. There was something so dizzyingly delicious about feeling in control.

Of course, in reality, she was far from that. She was decidedly *out* of control. But liberatingly so. She needed to do this more than anything she'd done in her life before. Lewis was going to give her back her self-esteem, her confidence, her very soul. He was going to revitalise her spirits and recharge her batteries. He was going to make her feel like a real woman again.

She found it surprisingly easy to free him from his clothes, marvelling at the way her non-fumbling fingers handled him so naturally, and so expertly. Not a hint of revulsion rose to spoil her skilful stroking. It was as if another person were inhabiting her body, a wildly uninhibited, chillingly expert woman of the world.

'Olivia,' Lewis choked out when her head began to descend.

She stopped and looked straight at him.

'It's all right,' she said, and smiled. 'Stop worrying. I won't let you come.'

Lewis was deathly silent after that, except for the small scratching noises his nails made on the leather as his fingers curled over and over.

'Now stay right where you are,' she murmured at last, pushing her hair back from her face and sitting upright. 'Promise me you won't move, now.'

His expression was disbelieving when she abandoned him, his eyes widening when she hitched up her skirt and peeled off her stockings and panties. Olivia wallowed in the way he ogled her legs. She didn't take off her skirt, finding a decidedly erotic charge in being nude underneath it. She didn't take off her blouse, either. That could wait.

Turning away from Lewis's galvanised gaze, she refilled her glass with champagne and took a deep swallow, just in case the wonderful effect of the alcohol began to wear off.

Bringing the glass with her, she returned to straddle Lewis's lap with her knees, glad now that her conservative skirt was not too tight. Even so, it rode up her thighs quite a way to accommodate her position. Staying kneeling upwards so that their bodies weren't actually contacting, she tilted the champagne to her lips once more.

'I think I might need some of that,' Lewis muttered hoarsely.

'Be my guest,' she said, and handed him the glass. He drained it, then dropped it over the back of the sofa to clatter against the other discarded glass.

'I have to warn you,' he said thickly, 'that I don't have any protection on me.'

'I noticed that,' she said with a dry little smile, and started undoing the buttons on her blouse.

'This is crazy, Olivia.'

'Calm down, boss. This is good old Olivia here. Do you think I'd ever be a health hazard?'

'Not usually…'

'Nicholas always used condoms,' she elaborated ruefully. 'I also started on the pill last month. I was just about to trust Nicholas, you see. Silly me! But not to worry. I trust *you*, Lewis. You have honour.'

'Honour! My God, do you think this is having honour—letting you do this when I know you're drunk, not to mention on some crazy rebound trip?'

'Don't underestimate your attractiveness, Lewis,' she purred. 'How do you know I'm not doing this because I've always fancied you like mad, but controlled myself because you seemed happily married? How do you know I haven't fantasised about you every day these past six months, that I haven't thought about you making love to me in your laboratory, or on your desk, or right here like this, with you buried deep inside me and my breast on your mouth?'

She watched him lose it then, the wildest, most primitive expression filling his face.

Knocking her hands aside, he ripped open her blouse and pushed up her bra to reveal her full, hard-tipped breasts. His hands were rough on her, his mouth hungry as he laved the nearest nipple with his tongue. Olivia tipped her head back with a low, sensual moan, her hair falling away from the arched curved of her spine. Sucking the whole aureole solidly in his mouth, Lewis pushed her skirt up to her waist, positioned himself at the entrance to her body then pulled her sharply downwards.

Olivia gasped. She wasn't sure why men liked this

position so much but she finally saw its attractions for the woman. Never had she felt so filled, her flesh totally impaled on his. Instinctively and voluptuously, she began to move, rising and falling upon him in the most incredibly pleasurable fashion.

All thought of Nicholas and revenge disappeared in the face of what was the most mind-blowing sexual experience of her life. Lewis was gripping her buttocks, squeezing them hard, urging her to a more vigorous rhythm. She obliged, her movements gradually growing more frantic.

Her head was spinning, her body burning. She could not find enough air for her pounding heart. Her mouth fell open and her cries overrode Lewis's ragged breathing, a high keening sound which ended when the first spasm struck. Olivia sucked in sharply, her head snapping forward. Immediately, Lewis groaned and arched upwards, his flesh pulsating and pumping deep within her.

Olivia could actually feel her own flesh contracting around him, squeezing him, milking him. The sensations nearly took her head off. Eventually, he sagged beneath her and slumped back against the chesterfield.

Olivia stared at his still gasping mouth and tightly shut eyes, then down at her own semi-naked self. Gradually, her nerve-endings stopped screaming and a wave of satiation flooded her body, bringing her down from her sexual high with the suddenness of a wet sponge thrown in her face. A sickening reality replaced the wild exhilaration she'd been feeling a minute before and a cold clammy sweat broke out all over her body.

Dear God, what had she *done*?

Her stomach started churning over and over. Battling hysteria, she yanked her bra down over her breasts then struggled to do up her blouse. Bile rose into her throat and she knew she was going to be sick.

She barely made it to Lewis's private washroom, just managing to lock the door behind her before she was violently ill into the toilet bowl. Even after Olivia was sure everything she'd eaten and drunk that day had left her body, more spasms struck. Beads of perspiration dotted her forehead as she hunched over in agony.

For several pain-racked minutes Olivia thought she might die. She wished she *would* die. Then she would never have to go out of this room and face Lewis again.

Her hand shook when she finally reached to flush the toilet. Moaning, she staggered over to the washbasin where she rinsed her mouth out with water, before sinking down into a heap on the cold tiled floor. She was huddled there, her head leaning against the vanity, when there was a thumping on the door.

'Are you all right, Olivia?'

All right! How could she possibly be all right after what she'd just done? The shame of it all brought tears to her eyes and the most awful tightness to her chest.

'Olivia?'

'Go away,' she choked out. 'Just go away.'

'Don't be silly. You're ill. I'm staying.'

'If you don't go right now,' she screamed at him, 'I...I don't know what I'll do!'

He sighed. 'I see. I had a feeling you'd regret things afterwards. Hell, I regret them myself. But damn it all, Olivia, you made it impossible for me to stop you.'

'Please,' she begged, squeezing her eyes shut. 'I...I don't want to talk about it.'

'You want to forget it ever happened; is that it?'

'Yes.'

'I'm not sure I can do that.'

'You *have* to. Or I...I'll resign.'

'Resign!'

'Yes.'

'I don't want you to resign,' he muttered. 'All right, I'll go, if that will make you feel better. Promise me you'll call yourself a taxi. Pay for it out of the petty cash tin.'

Olivia grimaced. 'I'll pay for it myself, thank you very much. I don't need to be rewarded for what happened just now. I've never been so disgusted with myself in my life.'

'It takes two to tango, Olivia,' he said. 'I'm as guilty as you are, if guilt is the word.'

'What other word is there?'

'Need, perhaps.'

'Need?'

'Yes. But we can talk about that another day. You're not in a fit state to discuss the complexities of life at this moment.'

'Just go, for pity's sake!'

'All right,' he said. 'I can see you're too upset to think straight just now. But I'll call you at home in the morning. Then we can talk about what just happened without the heat and emotion of the moment, okay?'

'Okay,' she mumbled.

'Good girl.'

Good girl? He had to be joking. Her behaviour just now had been appalling. Lewis had nothing to feel guilty about. It hadn't been *him* taking advantage of her drunkenness. It had been *her*, taking advantage of his no doubt frustrated state. Olivia was well aware Lewis hadn't even *looked* at another woman since his marriage broke up. If he had, there would have been phone calls toing and froing, not to mention other evidence. He certainly wouldn't have been working back late every night, and sometimes all night.

No, he'd been living a celibate life since Dinah left him, yet he was a normal red-blooded man in the prime of his life. His inability to resist his sozzled secretary's provocative and quite aggressive sexual attentions had been perfectly understandable. No, the shame and the guilt was all hers, right down the line. It was generous of the man to find excuses for her. She didn't deserve such consideration.

'Tell me again you'll be all right,' he persisted unhappily at the door.

'I'll be all right,' she said weakly, then sniffled, tears now running down her cheeks and dripping off her nose.

'I'm sorry, Olivia. You don't sound all right. I couldn't live with myself if I left you like this. Let me in.'

'No,' she sobbed. 'I can't.'

'So be it.'

Olivia gaped as, with an almighty cracking noise, Lewis broke down the door.

CHAPTER THREE

'DAMN and blast!' Lewis groaned, rubbing his shoulder. 'That always seems so easy in the movies.'

Despite grimacing with pain, he still bent and scooped up a speechless Olivia from the floor. She was awed by his gentle consideration as he carried her from the small washroom, angling her carefully past the mangled door before laying her softly down on the chesterfield. Snatching some tissues from his desktop, he dabbed at her damp cheeks and still wet mouth, picking out a long strand of hair from where it had caught between her lips.

'I'll get you a glass of water,' he said gently, and hurried back to the washroom.

Unfortunately, his absence brought Olivia's mind back to the scene of the crime, so to speak. The sight of her shoes and underwear on the floor near his desk made her groan. Memories flooded in of the things she had done and said.

Her heart twisting, she rolled over, buried her face into the black studded leather and burst into fresh tears.

The chesterfield dipped behind her, and she felt Lewis's hand on her trembling shoulder.

'Please don't, Olivia. God, I can't bear to see you like this.'

'I...I'm sorry,' she blubbered.

'It's not *you* who should be apologising.'

Olivia heard his guilt and felt terrible. With a great effort of will she pulled herself together and rolled over to face him. 'But it wasn't your fault, Lewis.'

'Yeah, right.'

His eyes dropped from hers, his shoulders sagging.

Olivia took the glass of water he was holding and drank deeply, using the time it took to empty the glass to collect herself, and her thoughts. She supposed she could keep indulging herself and totally fall apart. Or she could face what she'd done, honestly and without melodrama, and try to go on from there.

The temptation to just throw in the towel was strong, she had to admit. After all, what was the point in going on? The future she'd been working for and planning towards had no hope of being revived. Yvette had seen to that. Olivia knew it would take ages before she could trust her heart to another man. If ever.

Olivia was a very careful person.

When she was sober, that was.

Olivia gulped down the last of the water and came to a decision. Lewis didn't deserve her adding to his guilt in this matter. She could at least pretend she was all right for now, even if it wasn't so.

There was no doubt in her mind, however, that she would have to resign. How could she possibly face Lewis day after day in this very office? How could she stop the memory of this afternoon from undermining both her own self-respect and the respect her boss once had for her?

Still...the resigning could wait till after the

Christmas break. Frankly, she was far too fragile to do anything at the moment except go back to her flat and go to bed.

Alone.

But first she had to make Lewis feel better about his part in all this.

'Thank you,' she said quietly, and handed him back the empty glass.

His eyes lifted to search her face. 'Are you going to be all right, Olivia?'

'Yes, of course,' she said, although her smile was small and wan. 'I'm just being a typical woman.'

'Oh, no,' he said, shaking his head. 'You're far from being a typical woman.'

Olivia blushed fiercely and Lewis groaned. 'That's not what I meant, damn it! Hell, I can't seem to do anything right.'

'I think you've done a *lot* of things right, Lewis. Not many men would be as considerate or caring in the same circumstances. Believe me when I say I don't blame you for a single thing.'

'That's because you're not in my body.'

Olivia decided to leave that one well and truly alone. 'What's done is done,' she said wearily. 'I think we're *both* being far too hard on ourselves.'

The corner of Lewis's mouth lifted in a wry expression. 'Naturally. We're human beings. But perhaps you're right. Enough is enough. I'd better take you home now. You still look a little green around the gills.'

Olivia didn't doubt it. She felt dreadful. Alcohol poisoning, probably. Either that or some of the seafood she'd devoured with gay abandon on her champagne high might have harboured some gut-raising bacteria.

'I'll bring the car round to the side door,' Lewis offered, 'and meet you there in…say…five minutes?'

Olivia was grateful for the opportunity to retrieve her underwear in private, although the action of pulling them on sent her back to that unbelievable moment when she'd taken them off. Had that really been her, that incredibly bold and sexy woman who'd held Lewis in thrall? He hadn't been able to take his eyes off her, hadn't been able to stop himself from wanting her.

Olivia shuddered violently. She still could not believe what she'd done. Looking back, it was as if it had been some other person saying and doing those things.

Shaking her head, she leant against the desk while she angled her feet back into her shoes then stuffed the ends of her blouse back into her skirt. When she walked out to her own office the first thing she saw was the black bow she'd so recklessly pulled out of her hair all those hours earlier. Groaning, she shoved the painful reminder into her handbag, swept up her jacket from the back of her chair and hurried out of the room.

Lewis was waiting for her by the side door, sitting behind the wheel of his sleek navy Fairlane Ghia. Spotting her, he was out of the car in a flash.

'I was keeping the air-conditioning running,' he said as he steered her gently over to the passenger door. 'You might have to give me directions. I know you live in Gladesville somewhere, but I'm not sure of the address.'

'Just head down Victoria Road,' she said wretchedly while he settled her in the passenger seat and buckled the seat belt for her. When his arm twice brushed across her still aching breasts she flinched, then froze. 'I...I'll tell you where to turn,' she said stiffly.

Thank God it was only about a fifteen-minute drive at this time of day. The thought of going anywhere in a car with her dangerously rolling stomach was horrendous, the thought of having to bear much more of Lewis's solicitous attentions even worse.

The urge to scream at him was intense. Yet why should she want to do that? It was Nicholas she should be screaming at. *He* was the bastard, not her boss.

Somehow she got through the next quarter of an hour, but when the Fairlane slid quietly into the kerb outside her block of flats she exhaled deeply, which brought a sharp sideways glance from Lewis.

'I'm coming up with you,' he announced baldly.

Her head whipped round, her expression pained. 'Oh, no, Lewis, please don't. I...I just want to be alone.'

'I don't want any arguments, Olivia.'

Groaning, she closed her eyes. Olivia knew her boss could be stubborn. And quite forceful at times. She could admire such qualities at work, but not here, and not now.

Time for a little forcefulness of her own.

Steeling her still queasy stomach, she faced him

with an equally stubborn expression. 'I'm sorry, Lewis, but we're not at work now, and you'll just have to take no for an answer. If you're worried I might do something silly, then don't. I'm made of tougher stuff than that.'

'We all have moments of weakness, Olivia,' he said quietly, and she wondered if he was talking about what had happened earlier, or how he had felt when his wife left him. 'It's not good to be alone,' he added tellingly, 'when you're this unhappy.'

'I won't be alone,' she told him. 'At least...not for long. I'm going home tomorrow for the entire Christmas break.'

'Where's home?' he asked, then shook his head in exasperation. 'God, I don't even know that, do I? I don't know much about you at all. You've been my private and personal secretary for eighteen months and I know no more about you than I would a temp. Why is that, Olivia? Is that your fault, or mine?'

She shrugged. 'If you recall, when you hired me I was warned not to dress too flashily and not to be too familiar in my manner towards you. Your wife didn't care for your last secretary's forwardness, remember?'

'Yes, I remember,' he said ruefully.

'That's the only reason I told you about my relationship with Nicholas—because I thought it might put Dinah's mind at rest about any possible intentions she might think I secretly harboured towards you.'

'And why you never do yourself up much for work, perhaps?'

'In a way.'

'What does that mean?'

'It actually suits me to dress the way I do,' she told him with a tight, dry little smile. 'It's cheap.'

Lewis frowned. 'Cheap?'

Olivia almost laughed. 'That's something you should have worked out about me, Lewis. I'm cheap. Oh, not in the way I was cheap today, though God knows that was cheap to end all cheaps. But cheap meaning money. In other words, I'm tight-fisted. Stingy. Penny-pinching. I have a penchant for budgets, you see. And savings. And lists. Oh, yes, I'm a great list-maker.

'But my worst sin of all,' she swept on, 'is that I'm boring. According to my recently defunct fiancé, I don't have a spontaneous, impulsive bone in my body. That's why he left me in favour of a fantastic, fun-loving free spirit named Yvette who does all sorts of exciting things to him, things boring old Olivia would never do in a million years!

'But he was wrong, wasn't he?' She flashed Lewis a sickly smile, near hysteria hiding behind its savage sweetness. 'I *can* do those things. And in an office, no less. Nicholas would have been surprised, don't you think?'

'I think you should forget about Nicholas,' Lewis advised.

'Oh, I will. In time. I'm going in now, Lewis. Alone. Sorry I didn't get you anything for Christmas. I meant to buy something today, but today didn't turn out quite like I'd planned. *Nothing* lately is turning out quite like I planned. Do have a happy Christmas and a well deserved break. Not that you will. I know you'll spend the next five weeks in your laboratory, inventing more marvellous new products for your All Woman line. But that's not work to you, is it? That's your pleasure. I'm rattling on, aren't I? Sorry. I'm fine. Truly. This time tomorrow I'll be on the train home. Funnily enough, I'm almost looking forward to it. Didn't think I ever would. Christmas at home is always a madhouse. Maybe this year I'll fit right in.

'See you in five weeks, boss,' she added as she scrambled out of the car.

Olivia waved him off with a plastic smile on her face. Yes, she *would* see him again in five weeks. With her resignation letter in tow. Her conscience demanded she stay on for the four weeks' notice required in her contract, but that was as much as she could cope with.

It would be difficult to face him every day, but she would manage. And she would find Lewis a replacement who wouldn't give him any trouble, a nice, efficient, sensible, mature woman. Married, preferably. Happily married.

Poor Lewis hadn't had much luck with his secretaries lately. First, an oversexed blonde trying to catch herself a meal-ticket for life, then an undersexed brunette trying to prove she could be a right raver when required.

The right raver felt anything but as she made her way on glass legs up the stairs of the plain red-brick building to her ancient and tiny second-floor flat. Her head was pounding and her stomach on the roll again. She just made it to the bathroom before being sick once more.

After her stomach was well and truly empty, she

stripped and stood under the shower for ages, trying to wash the various smells from her body.

Feeling only marginally better but a lot cleaner, she finally emerged, dried herself, dragged on an oversized T-shirt then lay down on top of her bed. After half an hour she abandoned the idea of sleep in the claustrophobic and stuffy room, and rose to throw open the windows then make herself some black coffee. Pain tablets didn't seem like a good idea on her heaving stomach, despite the throbbing in her temples. An ice-pack helped a little.

By seven, she'd managed a little Vegemite toast, washed down with some more strong black coffee. Afterwards, she tried to pack, but in the end abandoned the idea in favour of television. Watching an episode of *Cracker* made her feel marginally better, her messed-up life seeming quite normal compared to the twisted, tortured lives in that show.

It also took her mind off things. It was eleven by the time she turned off the television and faced sleep once more. She was lying there, staring blankly up at the ceiling, when she remembered her pill.

Jumping up, she raced into the bathroom. Good God, what if she'd gone to sleep and forgotten it entirely? The thought appalled her.

Olivia swallowed Friday's pill and returned to bed where, once again, sleep eluded her. She began wondering what Lewis *really* thought of the way she'd acted. He'd made all the right noises afterwards, being a decent man. But he *had* to have lost respect for her. Perverse, since in her intoxicated state she'd thought respect was what she was looking for.

Well, she was going to pay for her folly, wasn't she? She was going to have to leave a job she liked and a boss she admired. People did pay for their sins, didn't they? You could do the right thing all your life, but make one mistake and your whole world could come crashing down. Not that her world hadn't already come crashing down before today.

Sighing wearily, she closed her eyes and tried to empty her mind. Sleep did come, eventually, but it didn't last. She woke shortly after two, sweating, and with stomach cramps. It seemed the consequences of the Christmas party hadn't done with her yet. One of the prawns or oysters she'd eaten must have been bad.

Crawling from her bed, she struggled along to the toilet where she sat for what seemed like hours. Finally, she made it back into bed where she tossed and turned till her next visit to the bathroom. By morning, she was pale and exhausted. Nothing, however, she vowed staunchly, was going to stop her packing and getting on that train.

The telephone started ringing as she was heading for the door with her bags mid-morning. After a momentary hesitation, Olivia kept on walking, telling herself that she didn't have the time to talk to anyone. The taxi was waiting for her downstairs.

If it was Nicholas, then he could go hang himself. If it was Lewis...well, the sooner her boss realised she wasn't his problem the better. She didn't want his pity.

And that was all it was. Pity. His heart still belonged to his wife. Any fool could see that. What had happened in his office yesterday had been sex.

Nothing more. Everyone knew men could enjoy sex without being emotionally involved.

As did drunken women, it seemed, whispered a snide little voice in her head.

The phone kept ringing all the while she was locking her flat door. What if it *was* Lewis, thinking he could have more of the same over the Christmas break? What if he hadn't fully understood that hadn't been the real Olivia making love to him yesterday? What if, underneath, he'd believed her when she'd said she'd always fancied him?

Oh, dear God...

Shuddering anew, Olivia hurried downstairs and into the waiting taxi.

CHAPTER FOUR

'I WAS right, Olivia,' the doctor said as he examined the small strip of test paper. 'You *are* pregnant. From the dates you gave me and the size of your uterus, I'd say about a month.'

Olivia's eyes blinked wide. 'But I *can't* be!' she protested. 'I told you. I'm on the pill and I haven't forgotten a single day.'

The doctor shrugged. 'That doesn't mean you can't get pregnant. The pill isn't a hundred per cent foolproof, even when you take it every day at exactly the same time. There are lots of hidden hazards. Antibiotics can create havoc with its effectiveness, as can certain other drugs. Even large doses of vitamin C have been suspected of rendering the pill ineffective. But the biggest culprit of all is gastric disturbance. Have you been ill at all during your last cycle? Any vomiting or diarrhoea around the time you had sexual relations?'

Olivia could have cried. In fact, she was very close to tears. Life could be so cruel!

'I can see by the look on your face,' the doctor said gently, 'that we have found the cause of this unexpected, and I presume unwanted, conception.'

Olivia just sat there, shocked and speechless.

'Are you in a steady relationship?' the doctor asked

softly. 'Or is this the result of a single unfortunate encounter?'

Olivia grimaced. What a tactful way to say a tacky one-night stand. Or, in her case, a tacky one-afternoon stand.

'I'm not in a steady relationship any more,' she muttered unhappily. 'I recently broke up with my boyfriend.'

'He's the father, then?'

'No.'

'Oh. Oh, I see…'

Olivia couldn't see how he could possibly see.

'Is there any hope that the father will support you and this baby?'

Olivia stiffened in her chair. 'I wouldn't ask him to.'

'I see. So what are you going to do, Olivia?'

'I have no idea.' It all seemed so unreal. And so unfair!

'Look, there's a very good women's health clinic up this way where they will advise you and explain all your options. Do you want a referral there or not?'

'Yes…no…yes. Oh, God, this is terrible! I can't think straight.'

'Why don't you go home and give this situation some serious thought, then come back and see me next week?'

'But I'll be back in Sydney next week. I…I have to go back to work.'

'Hmm. Do you have a regular doctor in Sydney?'

'No, not really.' If she needed to go to the doctor, she usually just toddled along to the local twenty-four-hour medical centre and saw whichever doctor was the quickest. In truth, she was rarely ill and had never felt the need to establish a relationship with just one doctor.

'I suppose I could go back to see the doctor who prescribed me the pill,' she said, her head whirling. 'She was a lady doctor, and very nice.'

'That sounds like a good idea. Lady doctors are usually more sensitive to girls in your situation.'

Girls in her situation...

Olivia winced at the wording. Being an unmarried mother was the last thing she'd ever envisaged for herself, and the last thing she'd planned on. She knew, first-hand, the consequences of a single girl finding herself in that predicament, and none of them were desirable.

An unwanted pregnancy had propelled her own mother into a precipitous marriage to Olivia's equally young and ill-equipped father, resulting in a lifetime of financial struggle. Her nearest sister, Carol, had fallen into the same trap and now, at the age of twenty-five, already had four children, none of whom she and her feckless husband could afford. Her boy-mad and silly sister, Sally, had only escaped a similar fate so far by sheer luck, in Olivia's opinion.

Of course, marriage was not the only course of action these days, but abortion wasn't necessarily the answer. It certainly wasn't for Olivia.

Her best friend at school had fallen pregnant during her final year, and her parents had pressured her into an abortion. Anna had still failed her exams then had a complete nervous breakdown. She'd taken an overdose of sleeping tablets which may or may not have been an accident.

It seemed telling that it happened on the day her baby would have been due.

Her funeral had affected Olivia deeply at the time, and for many years to come. It was one of the reasons she didn't have sex till she was twenty-five.

Suddenly, it was all too much for her and she stood up abruptly.

'Don't rush into any decision, Olivia,' the doctor advised. 'You have a few weeks up your sleeve. You're in shock at this moment. You might feel differently about the baby in a month or two.'

'Don't worry. I won't be rushing into anything.'

'Good.' He rose from behind his desk and walked round to place a comforting hand on her shoulder. 'Having a baby is not the end of the world, Olivia. You're not a silly young teenager. You seem an extremely sensible young woman to me. You'd make a very good mother.'

She stared up at him, for the first time thinking of the baby and not herself. But somehow it just didn't seem real yet, being a mother. She didn't *feel* like a mother. She didn't feel different at all.

Olivia thanked the doctor and left to walk slowly down the corridor to the waiting room.

Her mother was still sitting there patiently, her head buried in a *New Idea* magazine. Clearly, she was enjoying herself, wallowing in the glossy pages and the gossip. It crossed Olivia's mind as she watched her that her mother never had the money to buy herself such little luxuries as a magazine.

A great well of sadness washed through her. Was that what she wanted for herself? And for her child? A life of making ends meet, of doing without, of having to rent run-down houses and wear hand-me-down clothes?

Olivia looked over at her mother, with her worn thin face and greying hair. She was only forty-five years old but she looked much older. Yet she'd once been so pretty. The years of hardship had certainly taken their toll, this past year being no easier than all the others.

Olivia's father had been retrenched again, as he had eventually been retrenched from every unskilled job he'd ever had. To give him credit, he wanted to work, but it was becoming increasingly hard for him to find employment at his age. Not being able to find work had made him very depressed.

Christmas at home this year had been a lot more low-key than usual, despite the whole family gathering together. Olivia's own bleak mood had not been distracted as much as she'd hoped, although it had been soothing to be around people who she knew loved her. She'd spent the weeks since Christmas sitting in the rickety rocking chair on the tiny front porch and escaping into book after book.

Only at night had she thought of Nicholas, and, sometimes, of Lewis. Finally, she'd come to terms with Nicholas leaving her—she didn't want anyone who didn't want her back. She'd even come to terms with what she'd done with Lewis. Distance and time had lessened her shame and made her actions almost excusable.

She was contemplating going back to work at Altman Industries the following week and not resigning.

Or she *had* been. Before today...

Olivia's mother finally glanced up and saw her, standing there. 'Everything all right?' she asked, putting the magazine down and standing up.

Olivia smiled. 'I'm fine. Healthy as a horse.'

No point in adding to her mother's worries.

'I couldn't imagine there being anything really wrong with you,' her mother said as they walked out of the surgery together. 'You're looking far too well to be suffering from some weird wasting disease. So what did the doctor say about your missing period? Some problem with that pill you're taking?'

Olivia almost raised her eyes to the heavens as she gave a small prayer of thanks. She'd been racking her brain for a reason other than pregnancy. In a way, it wasn't even a lie.

'How did you guess?' she said.

'Interfering with nature is never a good thing. You should stop taking that pill, Olivia.'

'I intend to.'

'Let's face it, there's no reason to keep taking it, now that you and Nicholas have broken up.'

'You're so right.'

'I know this is no comfort to you, darling,' her mother said softly, 'but I never did think Nicholas was the right man for you.'

'Oh? Why's that?'

They reached the old grey rust-bucket utility her father drove and climbed in. Her mother shrugged as she started the engine. 'He was good-looking enough, I suppose. And quite smart. But far too young. And far too immature. You need a man who's already made it in life, who's very sure of himself and can offer you the security you crave. I know you, Olivia,' she added as she peered over her shoulder to check to see if any cars were coming. 'You will want your children to have the very best. Sally and Carol aren't as sensitive as you are. I understand how difficult it was for you, being brought up poor.'

Olivia's composure crumpled then. Tears flooded her eyes. 'Oh, Mum.'

Her mother's head whipped round, soft brown eyes alarmed. 'What is it, darling? What have I said? Oh, dear heaven,' she cried as she snapped off the engine and turned to face her distressed daughter. 'You *are* ill, aren't you?'

'Not ill, Mum,' Olivia choked out.

'Then what, for heaven's sake?'

'I'm pregnant. The pill, it seems, is not infallible.'

Olivia could hardly bear the sadness and sympathy in her mother's eyes. 'Oh, you poor darling.' And, leaning over, she gave her a fierce hug before pulling back and cupping Olivia's tear-stained face with gentle hands.

'This changes things, you know,' she said. 'You'll have to go back and tell Nicholas. Make him marry you.'

Olivia could have anticipated that reaction. It was her mother's only solution to pregnancy. Marriage to the father of the baby. She would never see any other way.

Olivia dragged in then slowly let out a steadying breath. 'I don't think so, Mum. You see, it...it's not Nicholas's baby.'

'Not...?' Her mother's hand fluttered up to her throat as her eyes widened. 'Then who?'

Olivia swallowed. 'Lewis.'

Her mother frowned. 'Lewis? Who's Lewis? Am I supposed to know who Lewis is?'

'He's my boss. Lewis Altman.'

Olivia was discomfited by the sharp look her mother gave her. 'Are you saying you've been carrying on with your boss behind Nicholas's back? Is that why he left you?'

Olivia sighed. 'No, Mum. It's Nicholas who's been carrying on behind *my* back with a girl in his office. There's never been anything like that between Lewis and myself. Not till the day of the firm's Christmas party, and that was two weeks after Nicholas left me. I'm afraid I had a little too much to drink and things just...well...they got out of hand. We both very much regretted it afterwards.'

'Really,' came her mother's dry remark. 'I'm sure that's a comfort to his wife.'

'He doesn't have a wife. She left him. They're getting a divorce.'

'Huh! I'd leave him too if he goes around getting his secretaries pregnant. Is that why the last girl left? The one before you?'

Olivia groaned. 'Lewis is not like that.'

'Then what, pray tell, is he like? You're acting like this was all your fault. I've never heard of a man being raped before!'

'Believe me when I say it was close,' Olivia muttered.

'Tommy rot! Was he drunk too? Was that it?'

'No. Only me.'

'Then he's just as much to blame as you are. Maybe more. This baby is his responsibility and he has to be made to face up to it. The least he can do is give you financial support. He's a wealthy man, judging by what you've told us. He can well afford to pay for his pleasure! So when are you going to tell him?'

'Not...not just yet.' Her mother just didn't understand. It *wasn't* Lewis's fault.

Her mother's normally warm brown eyes turned shrewd. 'Is he handsome?'

'What? Oh, yes. Very.'

'How old is he?'

'Thirty-four.'

'Well, well, well. In that case, I think perhaps you're right. Don't tell him yet. There's no point in scaring him off before he has a chance to fall in love with you.'

Olivia gaped. 'Fall in love with *me*? Mum, he's never looked at me sidewards in eighteen months. On top of that, he's still in love with his wife.'

'Not for long, I'll warrant. With men, it's mostly a case of out of sight, out of mind.'

Olivia rolled her eyes. Her mother had become very cynical lately. 'I told you. He's not like that. He's...he's deep.'

'Oh, come now, Olivia. He can't be *that* deep. Men seldom are. You're a very attractive young woman, when you want to be. He's already surrendered to your charms once. You did say *he* wasn't drunk, didn't you? The next time will be much easier. Before he knows it, he'll be head over heels and wanting to marry you. Then, and only then, should you tell him about the baby!'

Olivia could hardly believe what she was hearing. 'You expect me to seduce him a second time?'

'Whatever it takes. All's fair in love and war.'

'I am *not* in love with Lewis.'

'But you find him attractive.'

'Well, yes, I suppose so, but...but—'

'But nothing,' her mother broke in crisply. 'Think of the baby.'

'I *am* thinking of the baby!'

'Not enough, it seems. But you will. Babies have a way of bringing out the best in women. Nothing is too great a sacrifice for their welfare. Not that marrying a man like your Lewis sounds like too much of a sacrifice,' she added knowingly. 'If what you say is true he has all the qualities you should be looking for in a husband. Handsome. Mature. Established. Intelligent. And...deep, wasn't it?' she added just a touch tartly. 'Frankly, Olivia, it sounds like he's just what the doctor ordered!'

CHAPTER FIVE

'HAVE a good holiday, Olivia?'

'Yes, thanks, Pat,' she replied brightly. Pat was the security man on the gate at Altman Industries. No point in putting on a long face, either for him or for anyone else. Despite her mother's feelings on the matter, Olivia knew no one was to blame for the situation she was in but herself.

'You're looking well,' he called after her.

'Thanks,' she threw back over her shoulder.

She was, too. Perversely. Her complexion was glowing. Her hair shone. Her figure had never looked better.

Being pregnant suited her.

Olivia sucked in a sharp breath which had nothing to do with the incline of the pathway between the front gate and the main office block. Every time she thought of her pregnancy, everything inside her contracted.

She still couldn't quite believe things had turned out this way. She'd always been so sure her life would follow all those plans she'd made after meeting Nicholas, the list of goals she'd written down and which she'd hoped to follow. A well paid job by twenty-six, marriage by twenty-eight, a house bought and furnished by twenty-nine. Her first baby by thirty. And so on and so on.

Her plans hadn't included falling pregnant with her boss's baby at any stage. There again, her plans hadn't included Nicholas giving her the shove, either.

Olivia wasn't sure what she was going to do about the baby. Oh, she was going to have it. That was the only thing she *was* sure of. She just hadn't worked out whether she was going to tell Lewis or not. She'd rejected her mother's course of action as utterly unconscionable, and told her so. Two wrongs did not make a right.

She hadn't ruled out telling Lewis at some stage, but there were several good reasons why she'd decided to delay the announcement, and it had nothing to do with trying to get him to fall in love with her first!

One, he might try to talk her into an abortion. Olivia could understand why he might, but, even so, she preferred to continue to like and respect her baby's father.

Two, he might sack her on the spot, which would impel her to take him to court and expose the whole horribly embarrassing scenario.

Three, he might accuse her of trying to coerce him into marriage, which would make her want to sack herself on the spot out of contempt.

Four, he might write her a really big cheque, with the proviso that she never darken his office door again.

Olivia frowned. Now, was that an argument *for* telling Lewis, or against?

Of course some people would say he had a *right* to know, irrespective. He was the father, after all. Olivia appreciated that concept...in theory. But she believed the circumstances here were not the usual ones. She'd been the sexual aggressor and she'd assured Lewis that a resulting pregnancy was impossible.

Olivia would probably tell Lewis eventually. But later. Much, much later.

Meanwhile, she was returning to work and not resigning because she needed the money. Already she'd drawn up a new budgeting strategy to save up enough for a deposit on a small two-bedroomed unit in one of the cheaper Sydney suburbs.

Leaving Sydney was out of the question. This was where the work was, and she would always need to work, even if it meant putting the baby into child care.

She already had a substantial sum in the bank, and would receive a nice payout when she eventually resigned. She also had enough furniture to fill a small place and would search second-hand shops and advertisements to put together a nursery.

At least her new plans had kept her mind busy, distracting her from the many mixed-up thoughts which kept whirling in her head whenever she was idle. Hopefully, her mother's doctor would be right and she'd soon begin to feel better about the baby, or, at least, that it was *real*. Perhaps if she was suffering from morning sickness she might actually *feel* pregnant. Instead, she woke every morning, brimming with vitality and energy. Several people had already commented on how well she was looking.

She wondered if Lewis would notice this morning.

Olivia's stomach flipped over. It had been one thing to think of Lewis in a dispassionate and pragmatic fashion during her time away from the office. Quite another when she was about to face him for the first time since that awful afternoon, especially with the knowledge that she was carrying his baby.

Her stomach was in knots by the time she let herself in the front door of the main office block with her key. The only comforting factor was that the reception area and desk were still deserted. It was only ten past eight, twenty minutes before starting time. The office staff weren't in the habit of arriving early, especially on the first Monday after five weeks off.

Facing the rest of the staff was almost as bad as facing Lewis. If anyone made any caustic comments about her behaviour at the Christmas party, she would just die.

Fortunately, Lewis's rooms were at the far end of the longest arm of the L shaped building, well away from prying eyes and gossiping girls. Olivia was halfway down the long wide corridor which led past Sales and Distribution on the left, Marketing and Accounting on the right, when the side door opened abruptly and Lewis walked in. He checked his step when he saw Olivia, his expression startled, then relieved.

'Thank God,' he said feelingly.

Olivia's own step faltered. She'd forgotten how handsome Lewis was. How…impressive.

He was wearing a wonderful-looking suit that morning. Light grey, with a slight sheen. His eyes looked very blue against the dazzlingly white shirt and his deeply tanned face. Clearly, he'd been doing some outdoor activities over the Christmas break.

'Thank God for what?' she choked out.

His smile was lopsided, and wry. 'I had this awful feeling over Christmas and the New Year that you weren't going to came back; that I'd get some hideous phone call from your mother saying you'd quit and gone overseas, and would I please forward your severance check to some address in Angola or Afghanistan or wherever. You *do* have a mother, don't you?' he added, frowning suddenly.

She was taken aback. 'Doesn't everyone?'

'I mean...alive and well.'

'Mum's only forty-five,' Olivia said.

'She must have been young when she had you.'

'She was.'

Lewis's eyes washed over her. 'So how are you, Olivia? You're certainly looking better. Not so pale and drawn.'

'I *feel* better,' she returned, doing her best to act naturally. But she was having a terrible time trying not to stare at him, not to think of the life growing inside her, or to remember how that life had been conceived. But where before she'd been consumed by disgust at the memories, all of a sudden, in Lewis's very attractive male presence, she was thinking not of shame but of how it had felt with him buried deep inside her.

'Are you over Nicholas yet?'

'What?' she said distractedly.

'I'll take that for a yes,' he said, smiling.

Olivia dragged her mind back to the present, trying desperately not to blush. 'A partial yes,' she said.

'That's good,' he pronounced. 'We have a busy

year ahead of us, Olivia. I want the All Woman launch to be the best yet. I'll be needing you to work longer hours than usual. Will that be a problem? Naturally, I'll pay you overtime.'

Olivia hesitated. The money would come in handy, but the thought of staying back after hours with Lewis brought a rush of panic.

'If you're worried about what happened here on party day,' Lewis said brusquely, 'then please don't. I appreciate you bitterly regret that incident and want to forget it ever happened. I can't say I've forgotten it totally, but I'm certainly not about to jeopardise my working relationship with the best secretary I've ever had by referring to it again in any shape or form. Does that put your mind at rest?'

'Yes,' she said, and hoped she meant it.

But something seemed to have shifted in her feelings for Lewis. Where before she'd been able to ignore his considerable attractions, now, all of a sudden, she could not.

Her gaze returned to drink in every single detail of his handsome face. The perfect symmetry of his strong male features. The clear blue of his intelligent and deeply set eyes. His wide firm mouth with its deceptively sensual bottom lip.

When a frown drew his dark brows together over his classical nose, Olivia blinked back to reality.

'What?' she blurted out in a reflex action to embarrassment.

'You were looking at me oddly.'

'Oh. Sorry. My mind was a million miles away.'

'With Nicholas?'

'Not at all,' she said truthfully.

'Have you heard from him?' Lewis persisted.

'No.'

'If you do, don't go back to him, Olivia. He doesn't deserve you. The cheapskate didn't even buy you an engagement ring, I noticed.'

'That was my fault, Lewis. I told him I'd rather we saved the money for a house.'

Lewis gave her a disbelieving look. 'You know, you really are a unique woman.'

She laughed. 'Cheap, you mean.'

'Nothing about you is cheap, Olivia,' he muttered. 'Nothing at all. Come along, let's get along to our office before I start saying things I shouldn't.'

Such as what? Olivia wondered as she tried to keep up with his long strides. A sideways glance showed he was looking very annoyed with himself over something. His keys were out and ready before they reached the office doors.

And that was how the morning proceeded from there. Everything briskly and brusquely done. No more personal conversation. Just business, business and more business!

Olivia spent most of the morning bringing files up to date and sending for the hordes of people Lewis wanted to see. The national sales manager traipsed through, as did the accountant, then the marketing people assigned last year as product managers for the new All Woman line.

At twelve-thirty, Lewis left to have lunch with the executive from the Harriman advertising agency assigned to handle the launch of Altman Industries' new line. He was some new hot-shot, fresh out from New York, who supposedly had his finger right on the pulse. Harriman's had expanded considerably since Lewis had first used them. Late last year, they'd sent him a list of their latest television ads. Olivia had made a point of watching them at the time, and, frankly, hadn't thought much of them.

Shortly before three, Lewis came storming back through her office, muttering darkly, 'Stupid bloody idiot. Get the Harriman agency on the line for me, Olivia,' he threw at her. 'I want to speak to Bill Harriman personally. And I don't want any rubbish about his being at a meeting!'

Olivia's eyebrows lifted. She'd never seen Lewis in such a foul mood. When she put Bill Harriman through, she couldn't hear the conversation. Lewis was not the type to yell over the phone. He would be icily controlled. All she knew was the call was brief. When the internal intercom light buzzed on her communication system, she flicked the switch and picked up the phone. 'Yes, Lewis?'

'We're going to need another advertising agency. Any ideas?'

'Um...not off the top of my head. But I can make enquiries, I suppose. What exactly are we looking for? Conservative? Progressive? Way out? Already successful, or small and up-and-coming?'

'Small and up-and-coming. And run by women.'

'Women...'

'Yes, women! Hopefully women will know what will appeal to women, because those idiots over at Harriman's don't. They've totally lost the plot, the smug, arrogant fools.' And he slammed the phone down.

Olivia's eyebrows shot upwards. It wasn't like Lewis to lose his temper. When his intercom light flicked on again, she lifted the phone a little more gingerly. 'Yes, Lewis?'

'Sorry,' he said wearily. 'Forget what I just said. Finding a new advertising agency is not in your job description. I'll ask Walter. It's his responsibility as marketing manager. When he's narrowed the possibles down to a short list of three, then you can call them and get them in here for an interview. I'll talk to them in my office. I'm not buying any more expensive lunches for pretentious, free-loading fools.'

'Yes, boss.'

He sighed again, but she could hear one of his wry smiles forming down the line. 'You're very patient with me.'

'Now that *is* in my job description.'

'Olivia…'

'Yes?'

The silence on the line was prolonged and awkward.

'Nothing,' he finally muttered. 'Nothing.' And he hung up again.

Olivia found herself exhaling the breath she'd been holding as she too hung up. Was she imagining things, or had Lewis found that his feelings for her had changed too? What would Lewis do, she began to wonder, if she walked in there right now and told him she was having his baby? How *would* he react?

Logic and life suggested he wouldn't be too

pleased. Most men didn't welcome the news of an unexpected and unwanted pregnancy, especially with a woman they didn't love. Olivia didn't think Lewis's feelings for her had changed *that* much.

No, Lewis might be more aware of her as a female now, but he didn't love her. Neither was he likely to fall in love with her. As such, he certainly wouldn't be thrilled with the news of her having his baby. The only role he wanted Olivia to play in his life was secretary, not lover or wife. Her mother was way off the mark there. She just didn't understand men like Lewis.

On top of that, if Lewis had wanted children, he'd have had them by now. He was thirty-four years old, a chronic workaholic, consumed by his company and his creations. He didn't have time to be a father.

Olivia had always suspected Dinah might have left him over the matter of children, plus the long hours he worked. She probably hadn't felt really needed.

To give Nicholas credit, before their bust up, he'd always made Olivia feel needed, even if it had only been to organise his life. She *liked* feeling needed. It was almost as good as being loved.

The door to Lewis's office yanked open and her eyes whipped around to stare at him. He just stood there, hands on hips, legs aggressively apart, his handsome face flushed and furious. His hair was ruffled, his tie askew and his shirt sleeves rolled up. He looked magnificent, she thought. Like a wild animal on the prowl.

'It's no use, Olivia,' he growled.

'No use?' she repeated, her heart crashing against her ribs.

'I can't concentrate. I'm too angry. I've got to get out of here for a while. I'm going out for coffee. Come with me, will you? I need some of your sensible and soothing company.'

So that was how he still saw her, was it? Sensible and soothing. What a fool she was, imagining for a moment that he might now think of her as an attractive and desirable woman. Her mother had a lot to answer for, putting such silly ideas in her head.

'If you insist,' she said in a deflated voice, and reached forward to shut off her computer screen.

She stood up and was further chastened by his immediately looking away from her and giving his full attention to his sleeves, rolling them down and rebuttoning the cuffs.

'I'll just get my jacket,' he said, and was tightening his tie as he turned. 'If you want to go to the Ladies, go now,' he threw back at her. 'I'll meet you at the side door in a couple of minutes.'

'Yes, Daddy,' she muttered under her breath. God, now he was treating her like a child!

Olivia stared at herself in the ladies'-room mirror, turning her nose up at her reflection. Why *would* Lewis look at her with anything other than business in mind? Okay, so she wasn't wearing one of her severely tailored suits that day. Frankly, it had been too hot for a jacket and blouse. Maybe the office *was* air-conditioned, but she didn't have the comfort of driving in an air-conditioned car to work. She always caught the bus.

Still, her simple black dress was just as prim and proper, with its modestly rounded neckline, capped sleeves and sheath style that was darted in only slightly at the waist. The hem was just above the knee. Barely black stockings disguised her shapely legs. Her shoes were the same sensible low-heeled black pumps she wore every day. Her hair was secured in its usual black bow and her only make-up was a lipstick called Cocoa which she'd bought from a store for less than two dollars. Her short spray of Eternity that morning had long since worn off.

She looked and felt colourless. Sexless.

A glowing complexion and shiny hair, however healthy-looking, were no match for the superbly made up faces the other office girls presented every day. Their two receptionists always looked as if they'd stepped out of a fashion magazine. So did the other secretaries and female executives. Olivia had never envied their more glamorous image before, or their chic little dresses and short tight skirts.

Suddenly, she did.

But it's too late to change now, she told herself unhappily as she picked up her black handbag and left the Ladies. Far too late.

CHAPTER SIX

'PHIL BALDWIN was watching us through one of the windows,' Olivia said unhappily as Lewis angled the car down the driveway and through the security gate.

He slanted her a frowning glance. 'And?'

'He might think it's suspicious, us driving off somewhere together in the middle of the afternoon.'

Lewis snorted. 'No doubt he attributes everyone else with the same low sexual standards *he* lives by.'

Olivia stayed silent. She didn't want to add that Phil would have noticed their mutual absence at the Christmas party, since he was the one she'd been flirting with just before she chased off after Lewis, champagne bottle in hand. When neither of them returned to the party he might have put two and two together and come up with a nasty four.

'I know which way your mind's working, Olivia,' Lewis said. 'But thinking something isn't knowing it. Besides, Phil is a survivor. He would be well aware that spreading gossip about his employer could be hazardous to his health, not to mention his career.'

'I hope so.'

'Believe me, if he says a word out of place, he's out the door, and out of a job!'

'That would certainly stop the rumours, that would,' Olivia pointed out drily.

Lewis flashed her a startled look. 'Is this another side to you I haven't met before?'

Olivia flushed, and turned her face away.

'Don't go silent on me. I like witty women.'

'And I dislike complications in my life.'

'You see working for me as a complication now?'

'I see leaving the office with you in the middle of the afternoon a complication. My first instincts were right. I should have resigned five weeks ago.'

'I wouldn't have accepted it.'

'You would have had little say in the matter. It might have escaped your attention, Lewis, but an employee has the right to resign.'

'Well, *you're* not going to.'

'Aren't I?'

'Absolutely not. I forbid it.'

'He forbids it,' she repeated, smiling wryly. 'Well, that's a side to *you* I've met before. Did anyone ever tell you, Lewis, that you can be self-centred and stubborn?' As well as kind and gentle. And decent and honest. But she wasn't going to tell him that. He had a big enough ego as it was.

'My mother has pointed out these virtues in me,' came his dry reply.

'Not your wife?' she countered, and watched with a sudden and very avid curiosity while his mouth twisted into a rueful grimace.

'She might have mentioned them too, on the odd occasion.'

Olivia was dying to ask him why they'd split up, but her courage failed her at the last moment.

'Ah, here we are,' Lewis announced, and turned the

car into the car park of Carlingford Court. 'We should be able to find a coffee shop here in a public enough place to forestall the gossipmongers.'

They did, even if Lewis did choose a café with lots of private nooks. He steered her into one such nook. The waitress was by their side as soon as they were both settled, perhaps because they were the only customers in the place. Monday afternoons were not exactly the busiest of times for regional shopping centres.

'Cappuccino for two,' Lewis ordered. 'And two slices of that delicious-looking carrot cake you have in your display cabinet. Is that all right with you, Olivia?'

'Fine.'

The waitress hurried off and Lewis leant back in his chair, his blue eyes thoughtful.

'You're easy to please.'

'I'm always grateful for free food,' she said.

He grinned and she grinned back. Automatically. Unthinkingly.

'Watch it,' Lewis said, his smile turning wry. 'People might think you're flirting with me.'

'What people? This place is deserted.'

'In that case feel free to flirt all you like,' he tossed off nonchalantly.

'Flirting with the boss is definitely *not* in my job description,' she muttered, and looked away.

'Don't,' Lewis said softly, and she looked back.

'Don't what?'

'Don't turn away from me as though you've got something to be ashamed of. I told you once, Olivia, and now I'm telling you again. What happened between us was more my fault than yours. I should have stopped you. I've spent the last five weeks trying to work out why I didn't. I still haven't come up with a satisfactory reason.'

This revealing announcement only reaffirmed what Olivia already knew: that Lewis's feelings for her hadn't changed all that much. Clearly, he was still puzzled over how he'd allowed her to seduce him so successfully.

Such an admission was hardly flattering to her desirability as a woman. Neither did it give rise to any hope of a repeat performance, let alone the beginning of a real relationship.

Olivia was startled at how dismaying she found this realisation.

'Please, Lewis,' she said stiffly, and looked away again. 'You promised. Talk about something else.'

He sighed.

Fortunately, the coffee and carrot cake arrived just then and the awkward moment was broken. Olivia decided she was overreacting to everything today—she'd heard of pregnant women becoming highly irrational and emotional—and set about changing the subject onto something safer.

'What happened to upset you so much at lunch?' she asked while she emptied two packets of sugar into the cinnamon-topped froth of the cappuccino.

Lewis shrugged and began to lift his own sugarless coffee towards his lips. 'I guess I lost my temper.'

'I know that, Lewis. But why? What was it the man from Harriman's said that you didn't like?'

His coffee cup clattered back onto its saucer, its mounded creamy top wobbling dangerously. 'That idiot didn't have an original idea in his head! He thought he could simply copy what had been done with the All Man line and sign up high-profile sportswomen to endorse the products. He'd brought along photographs of several professional women athletes he had in mind. One was a lady weight-lifter who could easily have doubled as a man. Another was a marathon runner who looked anorexic. When I pointed this out to Mr New York, he said they looked fine to him. Well, they would, wouldn't they? He had two earrings, a ponytail and a lime-green shirt. I'm sorry, call me a male chauvinist, but none of those so-called women had the image I had in mind!'

'Hmm. You want to sell sex, is that it?'

'Not necessarily. I just want to sell the products. The very wording of the brand name calls for womanly women to endorse them, not scarecrows or beefcake.'

'Why don't you just sign up all the models in one of those girlie calendars and be done with it? Or the ones from the Sports Illustrated Swimsuit Edition?'

Lewis's eyes narrowed. 'Sarcasm, Olivia? Or feminism?'

'I just don't like stereotypes where women are concerned,' she said, 'especially in advertising.'

'You think I'm wrong to discard Harriman's?'

'No, of course not. Harriman Advertising has been riding on past laurels for far too long. They're overrated and overpriced. But if you're intending hiring an agency run by women I'd go light on that male chauvinist tack, if I were you.'

He was staring at her as though she'd turned into a little green man. 'You're amazing, you know that? Not only a mine of surprising information but intuitive too. It seems I haven't tapped into your full potential these past eighteen months or so.'

Olivia could not help thinking of the day he'd tapped into more than her full potential.

'In future, I'm going to consult with you more often on creative and business matters,' he raved on, oblivious of her turn of thought. 'In fact, I'm going to give you a raise and a new title, starting today. I hereby dub you my personal assistant. Better than secretary, don't you think? And what about another ten thousand a year? How does that sound?'

'It sounds like grounds for gossip,' she said ruefully. 'Phil Baldwin would make interesting copy of your giving me such a raise, Lewis.'

'You worry too much about Phil Baldwin,' he muttered. 'And you worry too much about gossip!'

'That's all very well for you to say. You're the boss. You're indispensable to everyone's survival at Altman Industries. I'm just your secretary.'

'PA,' he corrected her.

'Whatever.'

Lewis slumped back into his chair, his expression disgruntled. 'I brought you down here with me to soothe my nerves, Olivia, not to exacerbate them. Are you saying you don't want a new title, or an extra ten grand a year?'

She shrugged. 'I've always thought a title was nothing but empty wording, when all's said and done. But feel free to call me whatever you fancy.'

'Don't tempt me,' he said drily. 'What about the money?'

'Oh, I'll definitely be taking the money. I can't afford to look a gift-horse in the mouth.'

Olivia knew the moment the words were out that she'd put her foot right in it, so to speak. Lewis snapped forward in his chair, blue eyes intent.

'What do you mean, you can't afford not to? Are you hard up for some reason?'

Olivia had to think fast to cover her tracks. 'A little. Nicholas and I used to share the rent on the unit, and having to pay it by myself is putting a strain on my budget.'

'How much do you pay?'

Olivia hesitated. In actual fact her rent was a bargain for the area. It had taken Olivia months to find such a cheap place. Admittedly, the unit *was* small and on the top floor, facing west, which meant it could get incredibly hot and stuffy during the summer months. Nicholas had often complained, but Olivia had argued that short-term discomfort was worth long-term security.

If she told Lewis the real rental, he would suspect she was deceiving him over something, which was the last thing she wanted. Lewis had a doggedly obsessive personality when faced with a problem to be solved. She had to deflect his interest in her money matters. And quickly.

'Two hundred and twenty,' she lied, crossing her fingers in her lap in the way she used to as a child, whenever she lied deliberately, as though that would make everything all right.

'That's not too bad,' he said. 'Considering the area.'

Olivia almost groaned. She should have known Lewis wouldn't have thought that was too bad.

'You're not telling me the total truth, Olivia,' he said. 'I can see it in your eyes. That creep left you in debt, didn't he? I'll bet he ran up bills on your bank card, or some such thing, and you're just too proud to tell me.'

Olivia considered going along with Lewis's false assumption for a moment, but in the end could not. Nicholas might have turned out to be a bit of a creep, but he didn't deserve his reputation being defamed in that way.

'That's not it, Lewis,' she denied, then smiled a wry little smile. 'If you knew me, you'd know that no one—and I mean no one, not even Nicholas—is ever given the use of my bank card.'

'Then why are you so hard up? What's the reason behind these financial problems of yours?'

Your baby, she almost blurted out, but bit her tongue just in time. Searching her mind for some other reason for needing money, she came up with one based partly on the truth.

'My dad's out of work,' she said. 'I...I've been trying to help out.' Which was true. She'd offered her parents money several times but they'd always refused, saying they'd get by as they always had in the past. As a child she'd never understood their refusal ever to accept charity. But now she felt rather proud of their independent stance.

'How old is your dad?'

'Forty-six.'

'And what does he do for a living?'

'Whatever he can get. He's not an educated man, you see. Mostly, he works with his hands. But he's not dumb.'

'I'm sure he's not, if he's your father.'

She flushed at the compliment.

'What did he do last?'

'Worked down the coal mines in the Hunter Valley. Before that he was at the local power station. Before that, the steelworks in Newcastle. We've always lived in the Newcastle area, but we've moved around a bit.'

'I see. Then your parents don't own a house?'

'No. They rent a small place in Morisset. Why?'

'Just wondering if they'd be prepared to move.'

'To Sydney, you mean?' Dear heavens, surely he wasn't thinking of offering her father a job in the factory! That could prove very awkward indeed.

'Not necessarily,' he said. 'But possibly.'

'To be honest, I don't think Mum would like to move away from the Central Coast area,' Olivia said hurriedly. 'My sister, Carol, lives in Wyong and relies on Mum to babysit her children at the weekends while she works. Then there's my youngest sister, Sally, who's doing her last year at Morisset High. I don't think they'd like her to change school this year of all years.'

'Fair enough. Well, leave it with me and I'll see what I can do. I have a lot of business contacts who have branches up that way. Sometimes it's not what you know, Olivia, but who you know.'

'That…that's very kind of you,' she stammered, amazed and touched that he would bother.

'Don't canonise me yet,' he said drily. 'My motives are selfish ones.'

'How's that?'

His eyes were coolly unreadable as he lifted the coffee to his lips. 'Can't have my PA worrying about money, now, can I?' he said between swallows. 'Not when I want her mind on other things. Now drink up, Olivia, so that I can get you back to the office before all those wagging tongues have a field day.'

CHAPTER SEVEN

THE week raced by. Olivia spent most of Tuesday organising meetings for Lewis with the three advertising agencies Walter recommended, although not one of them was exclusively run by women. They did, however, have women working for them, and under Lewis's instructions Olivia told each agency to send over their best female executive for a preliminary discussion and presentation.

Also under Lewis's instructions, Olivia attended each one of these presentations, listening and observing so that she could present a female point of view to him afterwards.

Wednesday's woman got the thumbs-down from both of them. Her ideas had no originality, or feminine appeal.

Thursday's didn't do much better. She was an intellectual snob who irritated Olivia no end by being patronising towards all women consumers, thinking they would be fool enough to buy anything if it was packaged prettily. Olivia was glad Lewis agreed with her, not wanting to sound like a feminist in her arguments against that approach.

Friday's candidate brought a roll of Lewis's eyes as soon as she arrived.

Olivia didn't blame him. She wasn't enamoured of the grunge look, either. It certainly wasn't the right image for an intelligent advertising executive to present, if she wanted the All Woman contract. Her hair was so short, she might as well have shaved it. She had one earring in her nose, another in her eyebrow.

They heard her out, and, in truth, she had a vibrant and creative personality, but it was almost impossible to have faith in a woman who made herself look as unattractive as possible. She was also impossibly long-winded. Everyone at Altman Industries had packed up and gone home by the time she'd finished her spiel.

Olivia showed her to the door just after a quarter to six, mouthing a polite version of 'Don't call us, we'll call you' before returning to see what Lewis had to say.

He was shaking his head as she entered his office. 'Good God, Olivia, call me a male chauvinist again, if you like, but I prefer a woman to look like a woman, not an androgynous refugee from the worst second-hand clothes store in town.'

Olivia thought exactly the same, but somehow his comments irked, especially the bit about his preferring a woman to look like a woman. She shouldn't have taken it as a personal criticism, but she did.

'I don't think a woman should be judged by her appearance,' she said tartly. 'You wouldn't do that to a man.'

'Too damned right I would. And I did. You forget you didn't see that pretty boy I took to lunch!'

Olivia had to smile. Lewis had the same disdain as her father when speaking of men who didn't look and act like men.

'Speaking of lunch,' Lewis went on, levering himself up from behind his desk and stretching, 'I didn't have much today, and I'm starving. What I wouldn't give for a big plate of seafood, topped off with a couple of glasses of chilled Chablis!'

'Wouldn't we all,' Olivia murmured wistfully. She was still feeling remarkably well with her pregnancy, but she had this wild craving for oysters, which was perverse, since it was probably a bad oyster which had landed her into her present predicament in the first place.

'You like seafood?' Lewis asked.

'Love it.'

'In that case let me treat you to a seafood dinner. I'll take you to Clive's.'

'Oh, no, I couldn't let you do that.' Clive's was one of the most expensive seafood restaurants in Sydney. Down at the Rocks, it had a reputation bar none, and was frequented by the rich and famous. They *had* to be rich to afford to go there. 'It's way too expensive,' she said.

'Nonsense. Call it a reward for working so hard this week.'

'But you don't have a booking,' she argued, her mind racing to the eight o'clock appointment she had made down at the medical centre. Her lady doctor only worked week nights. Olivia supposed she could change the appointment to the following Monday night. Three days wouldn't make much difference. But she didn't want to.

The trouble was, she could hardly tell Lewis she

had a doctor's appointment. It would lead to more questions and more lies.

'You won't get a table,' she said. 'You have to book at least a week in advance at Clive's for a Friday night.' Saturday night was even worse. She knew this because she'd often booked Lewis a table when he was still with his wife. They'd dined there fairly regularly.

'We'll get a table if we go straight there now,' Lewis insisted. 'The crowds don't come till much later in the evenings.'

'Dressed like this?' Olivia protested anew, and with feeling.

It was all right for Lewis. His working wardrobe consisted of several elegant and expensive suits which would take him anywhere. The one he was wearing today was charcoal-grey, combined with a pale blue shirt and a snazzy tie in blue-grey and yellow.

Lewis's gaze swept over her rather old black linen suit which was always slightly crushed by the end of the day. A cream silk camisole *was* filling in the deep V of the lapelled jacket but it hardly lifted the outfit into something suitable for an evening dinner date at one of the smartest restaurants in town, certainly not when accompanied by her low-heeled black work shoes and bargain-basement black carry-all.

'What's wrong with the way you're dressed?' Lewis threw at her, his bewilderment seemingly sincere. 'You always look fine to me.'

Fine. His faint praise underlined how little Lewis really looked at her as a woman. She'd thought the

Christmas party might have changed that, but it seemed it hadn't.

She wondered how Lewis viewed that afternoon. As a momentary aberration brought on by drink? Maybe Lewis had already downed a few champagnes himself that day. Men always said that the more they drank, the better the barmaid looked. Maybe that applied to secretaries as well.

'Stop making a fuss, Olivia,' he went on irritably. 'And don't think I don't know the reason for it either, because I do.'

Her stomach lurched. 'You do?' My God, had her mother betrayed her confidence and told Lewis about the baby?

'Yes, I damned well do. Look, there's not a single soul left here to see us drive off together. You know what Friday afternoons are like here. Come four thirty-one and you could fire a machine gun around the other offices and not hit anyone.'

'True,' she said.

'So no more objections?'

Olivia could see no way out without, indeed, making a fuss. 'I think I should still ring and check there's a table.' That way she could slip in a call to the medical centre at the same time and change her appointment.

'Okay,' he said. 'You do that while I lock up my laboratory.'

Olivia raced back to her office and picked up her address book. The number for Clive's was the second under C. The first was for Carson. Nicholas Carson.

Olivia stared at his name, startled by how little the

thought of him hurt her now. Just a small pang of regret at the investment of time and emotion she'd put into him. She knew that if he came crawling back to her right now she would never take him back.

You couldn't anyway, you idiot, her pragmatic side pointed out. You're having another man's baby. No man wants a woman who's having another man's baby!

Olivia groaned, then dialled the number for Clive's.

Lewis had been right. They could give Mr Altman a table for two if he arrived by seven and left by nine. She accepted, though they'd be lucky to make it by seven. Her watch said a minute past six already. Swiftly, she hung up and dialled the medical centre which unfortunately didn't answer for several rings. When they did, she quickly told them who she was and that she wanted to change her appointment with Dr Holden to the same time Monday night. Luckily, that was fine.

'Great,' she said. 'See you then. Bye.'

'Everything okay?'

Olivia whirled round as Lewis strode into her office. Luckily, what she'd just said could easily be applied to Clive's. 'Yes,' she said, and snatched up her handbag, 'provided we get there by seven and leave by nine.'

'No trouble.' He took her elbow and shepherded her towards the door, pulling it shut behind them, the deadlock slipping into place.

'We have less than an hour,' she told him breathlessly as he urged her down the deserted corridor, 'to make it into the city, find a park and walk to the restaurant. The traffic will be bad and the Rocks area full of tourists.'

'Oh, ye of little faith,' he said, and smiled down at her.

Olivia didn't smile back. She was too busy controlling her madly racing pulse and telling herself not to set any store by a smile. A smile was just a smile and a kiss was just a kiss...

Olivia brought herself up short. How had her mind moved from smiles to kisses?

She frowned when that merciless mind moved on even further, filling with memories of where kissing Lewis had led that fateful afternoon. Swallowing, she tried to blank out the images of herself at her wicked worst. But how could you blot out images which were burnt into your brain?

Recalling her scandalous behaviour, however, brought a different reaction every time. Shame had long since given way to wonderment. Olivia almost envied that woman with her wild, wanton ways. *She'd* certainly made Lewis sit up and take notice, even if only for a short while. *That* woman wouldn't have worried about what she was wearing tonight. She'd have reefed off her jacket and shaken out her hair, with every confidence Lewis would be panting after her in seconds. He certainly would not have described her appearance as a lukewarm 'fine'. There was nothing lukewarm about her when in sex goddess mode!

Olivia's heart turned over at this last thought. She knew that staging such a transformation *without* the impetus of revenge and the Dutch courage of alcohol was out there in fantasy land. It was something to dream about in the dead of night, not in the land of the living, with all its harsh realities and hang-ups.

What good was that woman to her, anyway, now that she was going to have Lewis's baby? She didn't need Lewis to desire her so much, as to be prepared to support her in her decision to have their baby. She needed solid commitment to parenthood, not some passing passion.

Olivia's belief in a man's ability to commit had been dangerously damaged by Nicholas's defection. Which was probably why she was waiting before she told Lewis about the baby. She wanted to see if he was man enough to shoulder a responsibility thrust upon him by fate, not one he'd sought willingly. Better her baby remain fatherless than to have a half-hearted father who resented or neglected the child. Life was hard enough without feeling unwanted.

'You've gone very quiet,' Lewis said once they were under way.

Olivia glanced over at his thoughtful face and tried to guess what his reaction to her pregnancy might be. In truth, she didn't know him well enough yet to make an accurate judgement. He might have been her boss for eighteen months and her lover for eighteen minutes, but on a deeply personal basis she didn't really know him at all.

'Just daydreaming,' she said.

'You've been doing quite a bit of that this week,' he returned.

Olivia was surprised. 'Have I?'

'Yes. I couldn't count the number of times I've walked out of my office to find you sitting there, staring blankly at your screen. You haven't even noticed me behind you.'

She almost smiled. He sounded so piqued by her not being instantly aware of his presence.

'I don't like to see you this unhappy,' he added.

'But I'm not!' she denied.

'Oh, yes, you are. You definitely are. Which is understandable. Aside from the emotional trauma which is inevitable when a long-term relationship breaks up, no one likes to see all their plans ruined. I know you, Olivia. You're a planner, just like me. I have no doubt you're feeling pretty empty at the moment.'

Not empty enough, she thought, and began gnawing at her bottom lip.

'I was hoping the extra workload might distract you and fill the hole in your life,' he continued as he drove on towards the city. 'But, of course, that's a male solution. Women don't bury themselves in work when they're hurting. They like to talk. So feel free to talk to *me*, Olivia. I imagine you haven't got too many close friends to turn to at the moment. You never have when you've been a pair for so long, then break up. Other couples suddenly find you a threat and drop you like hot cakes.'

Olivia was moved by his caring and his kind offer, but stumped by the situation. As much as she wanted to get to know him better, he was the last person she could confide her worries to at that moment.

'I'm fine, Lewis,' she said. 'Really. But it's sweet of you to offer a shoulder to cry on.' Very sweet, actually. She hadn't known he could be so sweet.

'But you're not going to cry on it, are you?' he said drily.

'I'm not large on crying.' Which she wasn't. Before Nicholas left her, she'd hardly ever cried.

'So I've noticed. My last secretary used to dissolve into tears at the drop of a hat.'

Olivia smiled. 'From what I've heard, that particular female used a wide range of weaponry to get your attention.'

Lewis scowled. 'Perhaps she should have tried reverse psychology. That seems to work a treat.'

Olivia had no idea what he was talking about.

'I think a little distraction is called for,' he muttered, and reached forward to slot a cassette into the tape deck.

Olivia breathed a silent sigh of relief. Listening to music was infinitely preferable to walking the minefield of an intimate little chat with Lewis.

The crystal-clear voice of Sarah Brightman filled the car. Olivia closed her eyes and leant back to enjoy the wonderful melodies of Andrew Lloyd Webber.

They almost made it on time. If Lewis had been able to park close to the restaurant, they would have. As it was, they had to walk a couple of blocks and it was ten past seven by the time Lewis opened the black, heavily carved wooden door which marked the restaurant entrance.

Olivia tried not to gawk as she walked in, but, in truth, she wasn't used to such splendour in eating establishments. Burger bars and pizza joints had been the regular venues for her eating out with Nicholas. Real restaurants hadn't figured largely in their budget.

In fact, not at all. Olivia valued the money she earned too much to squander it on expensive menus.

She sighed appreciatively as she took in the richly panelled walls, the black and white granite tiles underfoot, the huge brass and crystal chandeliers overhead. It was as though they'd stepped back in time. A wealthy and very elegant time.

'This is so lovely,' she murmured.

Lewis glanced around as though seeing it for the first time. 'I suppose it is,' he said. 'But I only come here for the food. Good evening, Clive,' he said to the dinner-suited man who presented himself within seconds of their arrival.

Olivia had assumed he was the *maître d'*, but presumably he was the owner. About sixty, grey-haired and very formal, he would not have been astray butlering in some British mansion.

'Good evening, Mr Altman,' he said with a brief incline of his head. 'It's been a while since you graced us with your company.'

'It has indeed. This is Olivia, Clive. My…um… personal assistant.'

Olivia felt the urge to kick Lewis in the shin. How dared he hesitate like that, then give her new title such a provocative slant? It sounded as if there was something sly and sexual going on between them.

Hopefully, Clive knew of Lewis's pending divorce. She didn't like to think anyone imagined she was having an affair with her married boss. Which, of course, was exactly what Clive was thinking. She could see it in his eyes as they turned her way.

'How do you do, miss?' he said. 'May I take your jacket?'

She considered his offer for a moment. Despite the air-conditioning, the place was crowded and warm. But the thought of sitting across from Lewis for the next two hours in a skimpy satin camisole brought an uncomfortably squishy feeling to her stomach. 'No, I...I'll leave it on, thank you,' she said hurriedly.

'Very well, miss. This way, Mr Altman...'

Clive led them past the busy bar on the right and down the steps into the sunken body of the restaurant. A couple of the tables nearest the foyer were empty, but he continued on past them, taking them over to a far corner which afforded close to total privacy, courtesy of some potted palms and a delicate Japanese-style screen which should have looked out of place in the Edwardian-style decor, but didn't.

Clive's action in placing them there spoke volumes for his opinion of their relationship. Olivia wasn't sure if he was trying to hide them away from the prying eyes of other patrons because of discretion, or because he was hoping for a big tip.

After seeing them settled and pompously flicking out their white linen serviettes for them, Clive promised prompt attention from the drinks waiter, then departed to see to his other 'guests'.

Olivia was beginning to fume when Lewis laughed.

'What's so funny?' she said sharply. 'You know what he was thinking, don't you?'

'Clive thinks the worst of everyone who comes to his restaurant,' Lewis said with amusement in his voice. 'And he's usually right.'

'Well, he's not this time,' Olivia snapped.

Lewis scooped the serviette from the table and placed it across his lap before glancing over at her. 'No,' he said matter-of-factly. 'He's certainly not.'

Olivia should not have been pained by this cool statement of fact. So why *was* she? Was it female pride, rankling that Lewis could dismiss her so easily as a woman, even after what they'd shared?

Probably, she decided with some dismay.

Probably.

Her eyes dropped from his and she wished herself anywhere else but here.

'Olivia…'

She dragged in a steadying breath, then looked up. 'What?'

'Can't you forget him, just for one night?'

Olivia's eyes blinked wide. Good Lord. He thought she was thinking of Nicholas.

'He's not the only fish in the sea,' he went on. 'There are other men out there who would truly appreciate the unique woman you are.'

Olivia tried to see the kind encouragement behind the compliment, but could not. All she heard was the silent rejection within Lewis's words. *Other* men out there, he'd said. Didn't he know that the one man whom she wanted above all to appreciate the 'unique' woman she was was sitting opposite her?

His eyes were irritatingly sympathetic as they took in her frustrated face, which fired an even more frustrated reaction in Olivia.

I don't want your compassion, she ached to fling

at him. I want your passion. I want you to take me in your arms and tell me you love me. I want…

Olivia stopped the madness with a sharply sucked-in breath. My God, where had all that come from? What was happening to her?

'I should not have come here with you tonight,' she blurted out.

Now *he* was the one who was looking frustrated. 'Why ever not?'

'I don't like charity,' she bit out. 'Or pity.'

'Pity? You think this is *pity*?' He waved an angry hand around at the expensive restaurant. 'Pity comes a lot cheaper than this, Olivia.'

The arrival of the drinks waiter with the wine menu cut off their argument, leaving an atmosphere between them that was thick with tension. After a cursory glance at the red-leather-encased list, Lewis ordered a bottle of Chablis and waived any pre-dinner cocktails.

'Just bring the wine,' he said sharply.

The waiter left, unfazed by Lewis's brusque manner. No doubt he was used to overlooking the bad manners of rich male patrons.

This was another side to Lewis she hadn't witnessed before. The thwarted male.

'Now let's get this straight,' he ground out once they were alone. 'I don't pity you. This is *not* pity.'

'Then what is it?' she challenged. Let him worm his way out of *that* one!

She watched him open his mouth then close it again. The muscles in his jawline contracted as he clenched them tight.

'It's a boss trying to relax with a valued employee

after a very trying week,' he bit out. 'It's a man wanting to do something nice for a woman he respects and
admires. It's also a lonely human being, looking to
enjoy some pleasant company over a meal instead of
going home to an empty house.'

Olivia heard the bleakness in his voice and her
heart went out to him. She'd been so consumed with
her own personal problems tonight that she hadn't
given his a thought. Of course he was lonely. Very
lonely. No doubt that loneliness had contributed to
his succumbing to her seductive behaviour last
December.

Would her telling him about his baby alleviate that
loneliness, perhaps? Would it soothe the pain of his
wife leaving him? Give him something to help fill that
lonely, empty house of his?

'Lewis...'

'Yes?'

For the second time that evening, the wine waiter's
arrival interrupted them at a crucial moment. Last
time, his presence had simply put their conversation
on hold. This time, however, he saved Olivia from
perhaps making the biggest mistake of her life.

By the time Lewis had given his seal of approval
to the wine and their glasses were poured, she had
taken command of her dangerously see-sawing emotions. It was still premature to tell Lewis about her
pregnancy. She had to know more about him before
she set herself and her baby up for the cruellest rejection of all. Yes, better she raise her baby on her
own than to subject him or her to a father who would
reject, resent or neglect it.

No, telling Lewis could wait a while.

'What was it you were going to say?' Lewis asked as soon as the waiter departed.

'Say?'

'You were going to tell me something.'

'Oh, yes. I...er...don't like Chablis.'

He sighed. 'Then why didn't you say so? I'll get you something else. Sweet or dry? Red or white?'

'Um. Just a mineral water will do.'

'A glass of wine or two never hurt anyone, Olivia. It might relax you. Make you feel better.'

It might, she conceded, but everyone knew that alcohol was bad for a growing foetus.

'No, thanks. I think I'd better stick to mineral water.'

His glance was savage. 'So that's how it is, is it? You think that I've brought you here tonight to get you drunk so that I can ravage you senseless!'

Olivia was horrified. 'Good God, Lewis. Not at all! That's the furthest thing from my mind.'

'Well, it shouldn't be,' he muttered darkly. 'Because, believe me, it's not the furthest thing from *mine*!'

CHAPTER EIGHT

OLIVIA gaped while Lewis grimaced.

'I've really done it now, haven't I?' he said with a self-disgusted snort. 'Blotted my copybook well and truly. My only defence is that thinking something is not doing it, Olivia. If men were condemned on their sexual thoughts, then they'd all be on death row. I read somewhere that a man thinks about sex every ten minutes. That's an exaggeration of course,' he added, a rueful smile twisting his mouth. 'I'm sure it's only every eleven or twelve.'

A wildly sexual glint sparkled in his eyes as they raked over her astonished face, lingering for a few telling moments on her parted lips. Olivia snapped her mouth shut and his self-mocking smile twisted some more.

'I take it I'll have the pleasure of your resignation on my desk first thing Monday morning?'

Olivia almost groaned. Lewis's admission, plus his words about pleasure and desk, instantly recalled her own outrageous fantasy about his desk on that fateful afternoon. It hadn't been true...then. She could not claim such innocence at this moment. With Lewis's startling confession that he'd been desiring her, she could not stop such a scenario from sweeping into her mind.

Its effect was immediate. Her pulse rate soared, and

her nipples peaked hard under her silk camisole, shocking her rigid.

'I...I don't think that's necessary,' she said stiffly.

'I'm surprised,' he admitted.

'So am I,' she countered feelingly. She'd known she'd been more aware of Lewis's attractions since her return to work. But she could never have anticipated this stunningly sexual reaction to his own stunningly sexual admission. There wasn't even any champagne to blame.

Her mother would have been thrilled, Olivia conceded. But she wasn't quite so optimistic. On Lewis's side, he was admitting to nothing but strictly sexual desires. He'd also admitted to being very lonely.

Loneliness and frustration had obviously made him vulnerable to her. Affairs between bosses and their secretaries were common enough. The long hours they worked together bred an enforced intimacy which could be easily tipped over into something even more intimate. How much easier when that line had already been crossed once before!

Her mother clearly thought sex was a way to win men's love. Olivia knew differently. Men could separate sex and love without any trouble at all. What was startling her so much at that moment was that she'd thought women were different in that regard. She'd thought *she* was different. Now she wasn't so sure.

Had her confusing feelings earlier on tonight been driven by an emotional yearning, or a strictly sexual one? Was she falling in love with the father of her baby, or not?

Lewis's head tilted to one side as he studied her closely. Olivia feared her face was tellingly pink. She felt terribly hot, sitting there with her madly racing heart and appallingly erect nipples.

'Do you want my solemn promise never to make a pass?' he asked.

Olivia stared at him. It was a dangerously worded question. To say yes would be hypocritical. To say no…quite provocative.

'Would you do that?' she hedged.

'If I have to,' he said firmly. 'I don't want to lose you, Olivia.'

'I see.' That put his desire for her into perspective, didn't it? Hardly an all-consuming passion, if it could be so easily put aside.

Still, it was better than his not feeling anything when he looked at her.

'I don't think that will be necessary, either,' she said matter-of-factly. 'Now I think the waiter wants us to order…'

The evening was an unqualified disaster after that. At least for Olivia. Lewis seemed to enjoy his half of the seafood platter they shared. He also polished off most of the bottle of Chablis. Her own appetite was well and truly gone, spoiled by her inner agitation. She picked at the food, and sipped at her mineral water. Their conversation—what there was of it—centred on the safe subject of work. To her, it felt strained.

'Can you drive, Olivia?' Lewis asked her over coffee.

She looked up from her cup. 'Yes. Why?'

'I suspect I'm over the limit by now. So it's either you drive us home, or we catch a taxi. Of course, that would mean leaving my car in the city and I don't really want to do that. They sometimes get trashed. Naturally, I would pay for you to catch a taxi home from my place.'

Olivia sighed resignedly. 'Very well.'

'Believe me, this isn't some scam to get you alone at my place.'

Olivia didn't bother to grace that with an answer. Lewis paid the bill and they were soon walking briskly and silently back to the car.

'You'll have to give *me* directions this time,' she said when she climbed in behind the wheel. 'I know you live in Cherrybrook, but it's not an area I'm familiar with.' Understandable, since Cherrybrook was an exclusive and expensive suburb full of executive homes and yuppie lifestyles.

'You drive very well,' Lewis said ten minutes later. 'Yet you don't have a car.'

'Running a car is not very economical in the city. It's cheaper to catch buses and trains. Nicholas had a small car we used on the weekends. At least, he *used* to have a small car. He now drives a Porsche.'

'Let's not talk about Nicholas,' Lewis grated out.

'Yes. Let's not.'

'Some more music, perhaps?' he suggested drily.

'Good thinking.'

This time he chose the music from *Les Misérables*, which Olivia thought pretty apt for her melancholy mood. Fifty minutes later, he directed her into a wide, tree-lined street which featured some ginormous houses. Olivia should not have been surprised by Lewis's house but she was.

It was *huge*! A two-storey federation-style mansion which would have housed two families. It also had a 'FOR SALE' sign stuck in the middle of the huge lawn which rolled down to the street from the home's elevated site.

'You're selling?' Olivia asked as she turned the car into the driveway.

Lewis had already extracted a remote control from out of the glove box and zapped open one of the triple garage doors. 'Yes,' he said. 'By order of Dinah's solicitor. Still, it's far too much house for one man. Frankly, I never did like it. It was Dinah's choice, not mine.'

The lights in the garages came on automatically, and Olivia drove in. Lewis was right. You could have fitted six cars in there.

'You'll have to come inside with me briefly,' he said as they both climbed out. 'Unless you'd feel safer waiting on the front porch while I call a cab.'

'Don't be silly, Lewis,' she said sharply. 'I trust you.'

'I'm flattered.'

'It's not flattery. It's a fact.'

'Don't cast me as a hero yet, Olivia,' he said drily as he took her elbow and steered her towards an internal door. 'The night's still young.'

'And I'm so beautiful,' she mocked.

Lewis ground to a halt, and frowned down at her. 'Do I detect some cynicism in that remark?'

'Oh, come now, Lewis. Let's face it. I'm not the sort of girl a man can't keep his hands off.'

'I wouldn't say that, exactly.'

'So what would you say?'

'You're the sort of girl who makes a man think before he acts.'

Olivia nodded, her expression wry. 'Exactly. I make the men I'm with as boring as I am. That's why Nicholas left me. Because he couldn't stand what I'd done to him and his life. He told me he had to break out and live a little before I turned him into a spineless wimp.'

'You think being around you turns men into boring, spineless wimps?'

'I think I bring out the worst in them.'

'Now *that* I can agree with, Olivia,' he ground out, sliding an arm around her waist and scooping her hard against him. 'You're certainly bringing out the worst in me right at this moment.'

He cupped her chin with his free hand and held it tight. 'I promised you I wouldn't do this. But I can't have my secretary thinking her boss a boring, spineless wimp. I certainly can't have her believing I can easily keep my hands off her.

'Hell, Olivia,' he rasped, his mouth looming dangerously close to her stunned lips, 'it's been killing me keeping my hands off you all week. Every time I looked at you, I itched to take you in my arms, to free that glorious hair of yours, to strip away that perversely seductive façade you hide behind.'

Olivia's head whirled. Perversely seductive? What did he mean?

'Your very lack of artifice is arousing, do you know that? I look at your unadorned throat and I want to ravage it. I'm going to ravage it later. I'm going to ravage *all* of you, and you're not going to stop me, are you?'

He kissed her then, kissed her till she went limp with surrender. When he scooped her up into his arms and carried her into the darkened house, Olivia was way beyond protesting. It was as though she was caught in a fast-running tide, inexorable in its strength and power. To swim against it would be futile, and possibly fatal. She had to go with the flow. Had to.

'You want this too,' Lewis insisted as he swept up a staircase two steps at a time.

'I know you do.'

'Yes,' she heard herself whisper into the thick night air. 'Yes...'

CHAPTER NINE

LEWIS clicked on an overhead light with his elbow and Olivia blinked, both at the light and the room.

It had to be the master bedroom, because it was huge. Huge and elegant and distractingly feminine.

The decor was predominantly a dusky rose colour with a smattering of cream and pale blue. The carpet had a large floral pattern, and the wallpaper was dotted with tiny pink roses. The huge bed had a cream quilted bedhead and a flouncy pink bedspread. Olivia wasn't thrilled at the thought that this was the same bed Lewis had shared with his wife, but was too far gone to say a word.

He ground to a halt at the sight of it himself, whirled and strode from the room, going further along the upstairs gallery and into another bedroom. This time everything was predominantly green and gold. Much better, Olivia thought. She'd always hated pink.

He lowered her to the bed and kissed her anew, more tenderly this time, brushing his lips over hers and gently touching her tongue-tip with his own. She loved the feel of his lips on hers and the lingering taste of wine and coffee on his tongue.

'So sweet,' he murmured against her mouth before lifting his head and smiling softly down at her.

She blinked back up at him, and thought how wonderfully self-assured he was. Her mother had been right about that. Lewis was a man, not a boy. A man who knew what he was doing, both in life and in the bedroom.

'Who would have taken you for a tease?' he murmured, and trailed the back of his right hand across her sensitised lips. The resulting quiver ran all the way down to her toes.

'Of course, you don't know you're a tease,' he went on in a warmly amused voice, his hands busy on the buttons of her jacket. 'I do appreciate that. Which makes everything you say and do all the more effective. Just don't forget... I've already glimpsed the real you at the Christmas party.'

The real her? Olivia had never believed the person she'd become that day had been the real her. But maybe it was. She wasn't drunk now, yet she felt drunk. Drunk with desire. She could not wait to have his hands on her naked body.

'Beneath the tailored black suits and schoolgirl blouses you hide behind lies a very passionate creature indeed.' He peeled back the jacket to see the extremely unschoolgirlish cream satin camisole which provided no hiding place for her betrayingly bare breasts and shockingly erect nipples.

'Oh, Olivia, Olivia...'

She blushed as he smiled a wickedly sexy smile.

'Who could resist such a temptation?' he drawled, and bent to lave each nipple with his tongue till the satin was wet and clinging.

When he raised his head again, his breathing had quickened appreciably. So had hers.

'God, that looks incredible,' he rasped.

Olivia didn't know about it *looking* incredible, but it *felt* incredible.

His hands reached out to stroke down over both breasts at once, his thumbs rolling the satin-encased points till she began to wriggle and whimper.

'I almost regret having to take this thing off,' he muttered darkly.

He still took it off. He took off everything she was wearing till she was lying there before him, panting and naked.

'I won't be long,' he announced, and stood up to strip quickly, impatiently, giving her little time to appreciate his perfection before scooping her up into his arms once more and carrying her into the *en suite* bathroom.

'This comes a close third,' he said as he lowered her to her feet and began stroking his hands over her fire-tipped breasts once more.

'A close third?' she choked out, her mind reeling.

'Well, having you on my desk definitely comes first...' His hands splayed down over her tensely held stomach then curved around over her quivering buttocks. 'Followed by an all night session in my laboratory.'

Her face flamed at the reminder of the fantasies she'd thrown at him that day.

'Had you really thought of doing those things with me?' he asked thickly.

'Not...not at the time,' she hedged.

'But you have since?'

'I have thought of...of one of those things,' she confessed shakily.

His eyes narrowed. 'The desk?'

She could not admit as much, or even look at him. Her face felt as if it was going to suffer spontaneous combustion.

'No, don't do that,' he murmured, gently cupping her face and lifting her eyes back up to his. 'It's not wrong to think of such things, or even to do them. Not when you're with someone who cares about you. And I *do* care about you, Olivia. You must believe that. There's no reason for you to feel guilty about this, or to ever regret it. This isn't an act of revenge, or rebellion. This is a man and a woman reaching out to each other as men and women have been reaching out to each other since Adam and Eve. It isn't shameful or wicked. Sex is a God-given gift, bestowed on the human race for very good reasons, to be enjoyed, not worried over. It's Mother Nature, Olivia...'

So saying, he turned on the shower and drew her under the water with him, into a warm erotic world where her body was soon awash with the most mind-bending pleasure. His soap-slicked hands slid over her glistening skin, turning her this way and that while he caressed, and explored, and teased.

She surrendered herself totally to his will, closing her eyes and tipping her face up to the heated spray while his hands were busy on her body. Her back was to him when he bent his lips to her shoulder, and then her throat. His hands began rubbing up and down her arms in long, sensuous strokes and she could feel his erection pressing into her from behind, rock-like and urgent.

'Olivia,' he rasped against her ear. 'You said last

time there was no need to use anything. Does that still apply?'

'What? Oh, yes…yes…' She didn't want to talk, or think. She just wanted him inside her.

Instinctively and invitingly, her legs moved apart to give him access to her from where he was. He groaned, and, taking her hands, braced her against the wet tiled wall, the action bending her slightly forward. The water beat down on her back and she could barely believe she was just standing there, offering herself to him in such an erotic fashion.

His hands kneaded her tense buttocks, sending wild tremors rippling through her. When his fingers slipped down between her legs and inside her, a long low moan ripped from her throat. As exciting as she found his knowing touch, at that point, she wanted more, she wanted *him*.

'Yes, honey, yes,' he promised when her wriggling bottom and wild panting signalled her desperation and need.

She groaned at the feel of his flesh slowly filling hers, then again when he began to move back and forth with deeply sensual thrusts. The position found pleasure points inside Olivia that she hadn't known existed before and everything started swimming in her head.

'Don't stop,' she pleaded, and began rocking back and forth in time with his rhythm. 'Oh, please…don't stop.'

She groaned when his left hand splayed hard and firm across her tensely held stomach, then gasped when his other hand slipped down between her trembling legs once more. She came instantly, and so did he. Explosively. Exquisitely.

Olivia might have slumped to her knees at that point, but he was holding her upright and close, his arms wrapped solidly around her. His mouth moved to trail down her throat and across her right shoulder, kissing her skin as he rocked her softly to him under the shower.

'Are you all right?' he whispered at last.

'Mmm.' She could hardly stay awake under the beating heat of the water and the drugging aftermath of their torrid lovemaking.

'You need sleep,' Lewis said.

'Mmm,' she agreed on a soft sigh.

He washed her gently first, then switched off the water and pulled a thick cream towel into the shower cubicle. After some swift drying, he tossed that towel aside and dragged in another which he wrapped round her before carrying her back to the bedroom. When he pulled back the bedclothes and tried to lower her onto the cool clean sheets, she linked her arms around his neck and pulled him with her.

'Sleep *with* me, Lewis,' she urged huskily.

His smile was reassuring. 'Believe me, I intend to.'

'Good.'

'No, possibly not good, Olivia. But I'm going to all the same.'

'What do you mean?'

'We both know you're still vulnerable over Nicholas. You'll regret this in the morning. I know you will.'

'You said no guilt,' she reminded him. 'And no regrets.'

'That was before. This is after. That's one thing you should know about men, Olivia. They sometimes twist the truth a little when in the grip of lust. Now go to sleep. I'm going downstairs to see everything is locked up, then I'll be back to join you.'

Her heart sank as he tucked her in, then left the room. Had Lewis twisted the truth only a little, or a lot? Had he meant it when he said he cared about her, or had he just said whatever it took to get what he wanted?

In the grip of lust, he'd said. Was that what she'd been suffering from too? Lust?

She grimaced as she thought of all she'd allowed and welcomed in that shower, shaking her head at herself.

Yet there was no excuse this time. No champagne to blame. And no Nicholas, either. Lewis was wrong there. She *was* over Nicholas. Lewis was the only man who filled her thoughts these days, the only man she wanted, the only man she...loved?

Olivia frowned. She still didn't know about that, which was odd. She'd always been a person who was very sure of her feelings. But Lewis had her totally confused.

Was it the baby doing the confusing? Was that it?

Having thought of the baby growing within her, Olivia suddenly began to worry. Had their rather torrid lovemaking put the baby at risk?

Surely not. She recalled her sister telling her she

still had sex during her pregnancies. In fact, Carol had claimed to find it a particularly sexy time.

The baby would only be tiny at this time, Olivia reasoned. She was only six weeks pregnant and feeling very well indeed. She was being silly.

But her momentary panic had been telling. The baby was becoming real to her. She was turning into a mother. What next? she wondered.

The sound of footsteps on the stairs had Olivia curling up on her side and pretending to be asleep. She didn't move a muscle when Lewis climbed into the bed beside her. She didn't flinch when he turned his back on her and his naked buttocks brushed against hers.

Sleep did not come quickly. Tension did that to one. But come it did, and with it all Olivia's defences dissipated. So when Lewis began stroking her breasts in the early hours of the morning she wasn't in a fit state to defend herself from the desires he aroused. He turned her over and moved into her before she was properly awake, yet already she was reaching for him, curling her legs sinuously around his waist, and arching up into him. This time their mating was slow and tender, Olivia stroking down his spine while he covered her face with tender kisses.

Olivia was stunned by her emotional response to their coming together again, an overwhelming wave of affection and tenderness washing through her as Lewis trembled uncontrollably in her arms. She might not be in love with him, she conceded, but she cared about him a great deal.

And, hopefully, he cared about her in return. Surely

he hadn't lied about that. No man made love as tenderly as he had just done without some depth of feeling.

Or was that just foolish female thinking?

Olivia fell asleep in Lewis's arms, still confused and still unsure.

CHAPTER TEN

OLIVIA woke to the smell of coffee. It was teasing her nostrils before she'd even opened her eyes, making her mouth water. She'd barely put an arm outside the cosiness of the quilt when Lewis walked in, carrying a steaming mug.

Showered but not shaven, he was dressed in stone-washed jeans and a red and grey striped top, giving Olivia her first glimpse of Lewis on the weekend. It was a casual and sexy look, with his designer stubble and shower-damp hair.

'Good morning,' he said brightly. 'Sleep well?'

'Er...yes, thanks,' she said stiffly, popping her bare arm back under the quilt which she then dragged up to her throat.

Sighing expressively, Lewis placed the mug down on the bedside chest and sat down on the side of the bed. 'Come now, Olivia,' he said wryly, 'I think we've moved beyond that.'

'Beyond what?'

'Beyond embarrassment. We're lovers now, and there's no going back. You don't *want* to go back, do you?' he added, frowning sharply at her.

'Not really.'

'No regrets?'

'Not...not really.'

'Then what's the problem?'

Olivia sighed. 'I...I guess I'm just not used to you waiting on me like this.' And, picking up the coffee, she took a few tentative sips.

'Then I suggest you *get* used to it,' Lewis pronounced, setting sparkling blue eyes upon her. 'You'll find I'm a different guy out of the office. I *like* to lavish attention on the woman in my life. And you're going to be the woman in my life, Olivia. Make no mistake about that.'

Olivia was taken aback by this unexpected avowal. It hardly matched the way Lewis had acted last night. He'd made her feel that what she'd done in surrendering herself to him sexually a second time had been very foolish indeed. She'd gone to sleep feeling troubled. She'd woken still troubled.

'I...I'd like to be the woman in your life, Lewis,' she said carefully. 'But...'

'But what? Oh, I know I had my doubts last night. But they were more *your* doubts than mine, Olivia. I've thought about everything this morning and this is what I want.'

'Have you thought about what will happen around the office?' she said, doing her best to keep a lid on her growing elation. 'People will talk and snigger and—'

'They don't have to know, do they?' he broke in.

Olivia's heart sank. 'You...want our relationship to be a secret?'

'For the time being. At least till my divorce comes through. Personally, I don't give a damn if people talk about me, but I can see how gossip would hurt someone as fine and sensitive as you are.'

Olivia almost preened at the compliment. Fine and sensitive. They were lovely words. She could not have felt happier. Except for one thing...

Given Lewis's obvious intention to have a lasting relationship with her, she would have to tell him about her pregnancy sooner or later. She could not hope to keep their baby a secret for ever. Maybe sooner would be better than later...

'Lewis...'

'Yes?'

'The thing is, I...I...' Even as she opened her mouth to tell him, fear and anxiety rushed in to muddy her thoughts once more. He hadn't said he loved her, after all. He wasn't free to marry her, either. Maybe all he wanted from her at the moment was sex. Maybe he'd still try to talk her into an abortion!

'You don't have to say it,' Lewis said drily, and Olivia's eyes blinked wide.

'I know you're not in love with me,' he went on. 'I don't expect that from you at this point in your life. I understand how difficult it is to open your heart again so soon after you've been hurt. I have to be honest, Olivia. I'm not in love with you, either. Not with that blind, all-consuming passion which makes you put aside your usual common sense and rush into a relationship which you should have known deep down wasn't going to work.'

Olivia listened to his soothing sensible words and wondered why she wasn't at all soothed.

The doorbell ringing sent Lewis's eyebrows arching ceilingwards. 'Now who on earth could *that* be at this hour on a Saturday morning?'

'I hope it's not your mother,' Olivia said, dry-mouthed.

'I doubt it. Mum always shops on a Saturday morning. Still, she wouldn't object to *your* being in my bed, Olivia. Surprised, maybe. But not unhappy in the slightest.'

He rose and walked towards the bedroom door. 'Drink your coffee,' he threw back over his shoulder, 'and I'll go see who it is come calling so early.'

Olivia glanced down at her watch, the only article to grace her nude body. It was five to ten. Not all that early.

She heard Lewis walk downstairs, heard him open the front door, heard his irritated greeting.

'Good God, Dinah, what in hell are you doing here?'

Olivia didn't hear what was said in return, but her straining ears picked us Lewis's next retort as it echoed in the cavernous foyer. 'You can see the sign for yourself,' he bit out. 'I can't help it if the price you insisted I put on the house is way over market value. Property buyers aren't fools, you know. Not like some husbands.'

Olivia put down the coffee mug, scrambled out of bed and dashed for the bathroom. She could not bear to listen to the emotion in Lewis's voice for another second, could not bear to hear the evidence of where Lewis's heart still lay.

She snapped on the water and plunged beneath its hard wet spray. Letting out her hair, she grabbed a bottle of shampoo from the shelf and was furiously lathering up her scalp when she realised she was crying. Hot, stinging tears.

It was a telling moment for Olivia, that heart-wrenching moment when she realised she *did* love Lewis, loved him with that blind, all-consuming passion Lewis had obviously once felt for his wife, and which still coloured his life.

'Oh, God,' she choked out, and covered her eyes with her hands.

Big mistake!

The shampoo stung even more than her tears. Flinging wide her flooding, red-rimmed eyes, she tipped them up to the shower and let the water wash them clear. She stood there like that for ages and eventually the pain receded and some composure returned.

But it was definitely time to get dressed and go home.

Fifteen minutes later Olivia looked as if she was setting off for a day at the office. The buttons of her black jacket were safely done up over the saliva-stained camisole and her damp dark hair was slicked back and wound into a tightly twisted knot. She wasn't wearing any lipstick because she didn't have any up here with her. Her handbag was still on the floor of Lewis's garage.

Olivia looked dully at her drab reflection in the dressing-table mirror and wondered why Lewis wanted her at all. Compared to his glamorous blonde wife, she was a plain Jane.

From the top of the stairs, she could see that the

front door was closed. No sounds were issuing from downstairs. Either Lewis was outside talking to Dinah, or she'd left. Olivia hoped and prayed it was the latter.

On the way downstairs, she could not help but shake her head at her surroundings. Everywhere she looked lay evidence of extravagance and wealth, from the gilt-framed oil paintings gracing the elegantly papered walls to the huge crystal chandelier hanging in the vaulted ceiling.

Although exquisitely decorated and furnished, the house wasn't to her taste at all. Even if she had a lot of money, Olivia would want her home to look like a home—somewhere you could relax in. She could not imagine children in a home like this.

Olivia stepped gingerly from the plushly carpeted steps onto the glazed marble tiles, thinking you could break your neck on such a floor. She was just wondering which way to turn when a female voice drifted through an open doorway on her left.

'There's no need to skulk off, Olivia.'

Lewis's wife came into view across the expanse of cream carpet, carrying a pair of exquisite glass swans. Their deep violet colour matched her heavily made up eyes, and looked stunning against her white linen suit and white-blonde hair.

'Lewis tried to get rid of me by saying he wasn't alone,' Dinah said, her gaze coldly amused as it travelled over Olivia from head to toe. 'But, as you can see, that excuse didn't work. It only aroused my curiosity further, so I forced him to tell me the identity of his new bed-partner. Either that or I was going to go up and see for myself. For some reason, he didn't want you subjected to my sweet presence. He's in the garage, by the way, trying to find the boxes these came in.'

Olivia had never felt as small as she did at that moment.

'You know, I'm not often surprised, but I have to admit you've surprised me. Yet I'm well acquainted with the things ambitious secretaries will do where their bosses are concerned. But you had me fooled, all right, with your schoolmarm image. Still, knowing Lewis, you must be a hot little number once you get your gear off. He does like his sex, does Lewis. My only question is, what happened to the boyfriend? Did you ditch him once Lewis became available? Was that it?'

Olivia's temper began to rise with each question. But she refused to take the bait. 'I'll just go back upstairs till you've gone,' she said coolly, and spun on her sensible heels to start up the stairs again.

'If you think he's going to marry a little mouse like you, honey,' Dinah threw after her, 'then think again. You're just a filler till he finds wife number two to fit his five-star plan.'

Olivia whirled at the mention of a plan. Dinah was standing at the bottom of the stairs, her expression smug.

'What do you mean?' Olivia asked breathlessly.

'For pity's sake, you must know what Lewis is like. Impulse doesn't match his personality. He plans everything that matters to him. And, believe me, the choice of wife and mother to his children matters very much to Lewis. He wants his offspring to have it all, you see. Looks. Intelligence. Style. And good old-fashioned twenty-four-hour-a-day mothering.'

Dinah paused, possibly to let what she was saying sink in. And sink in it did.

'Contrary to Lewis's plans,' she went on ruefully, 'I wasn't prepared to give up my career on cue to stay at home and have his two perfect babies. I *am* only twenty-five, after all. I said I'd have them when I turned thirty but that wasn't good enough. So do you know what he did? He threw me out. Yes, your wonderful boss just got rid of me. Believe me when I tell you as soon as the divorce comes through he'll dump you, darling, and marry some pretty young malleable thing who'll do exactly what he wants, when he wants.'

'I...I don't believe you,' Olivia said shakily, and Dinah laughed.

'Which part don't you believe?'

'Lewis does...*did* love you.'

'Lewis doesn't know the meaning of the word,' she scoffed. 'He *wants*, does Lewis. Oh, quite passionately, I must admit. I'm sure he wants you, my dear, at least for the next six months. But don't ever forget those wonderful plans of his. Which means don't ever try to rise above your status as secretary-cum-convenient lover, or you'll find yourself discarded as swiftly and surely as I was.' Walking coolly over to the front door, she turned and threw Olivia a sickening smile. 'Tell Lewis I've decided I don't want these swans after all.'

Olivia watched, mouth widening, while Dinah quite

deliberately let the exquisite figurines slip from her fingers. She was already on her way out of the door before they smashed to smithereens on the marble floor, glass scattering everywhere. The noise was deafening as it echoed through the house.

Lewis came running, a couple of cardboard cartons in his hands. He stared, first down at the no longer recognisable swans, then up at his pale-faced secretary. Tossing aside the cartons, he leapt up the stairs to enfold her shocked and stiffly held body in his arms.

'That bitch,' he muttered darkly, and stroked down Olivia's trembling spine. 'She can't stand to see me happy. What in hell did she say to you?'

'She said…she said…'

Lewis pulled back to stare down at her, his eyes concerned. Or were they wary?

'What?' he asked sharply. 'What did she say?'

Olivia felt sick inside. 'She…she said to tell you she didn't want the swans any more.'

His laugh was harsh. 'What Dinah doesn't want,' he ground out, 'is for me to ever be happy. She's a vicious, vindictive bitch who doesn't want me any more, but doesn't want anybody else to have me.'

'She said it was *you* who threw her out.'

He snorted. 'Did she, now?'

'*Did* you?' Olivia asked, determined to have the truth, even while nausea swirled in her stomach.

'Not literally. I *did* suggest to her after our final argument that if she chose to leave for another extended buying trip overseas she need not return. By the time she came home several weeks later, I'd changed the locks and couriered all her personal effects to her parents' home.'

Which was the same as throwing her out in Olivia's opinion. She could see now that the emotion she'd heard vibrating in Lewis's voice this morning hadn't been a lingering love, but fury. Fury that this woman had dared to show up in his life again when he'd dispensed with her once and for all.

'Did…did you *ever* love her, Lewis?'

He shrugged offhandedly. 'I doubt it. I was tricked by a clever acting job. She turned out to be a totally different woman to the one I thought I was marrying. But let's not talk about Dinah any more,' he went on, his expression showing nothing but distaste. 'She's dead and gone as far as I'm concerned.'

Olivia stared at him. Dinah hadn't exaggerated. His estranged wife was not just discarded and dismissed. She was dead and gone! Olivia had recovered from Nicholas's betrayal, but she hadn't forgotten him or what they'd once shared. She *had* loved him, and still thought of him, sometimes quite fondly. He wasn't all bad. Just young and weak and immature. He hadn't known what he really wanted.

Lewis was a grown man. Ambitious and focused. He *knew* what he wanted.

Olivia began to shake her head in denial of the silly hopes she'd been harbouring about him. Dinah had been right about Lewis not wanting to marry her. His plans didn't include his secretary becoming his second wife, and the mother of his children. Which was too bad. Because she was going to be the mother of at least one child of his, whether he wanted her imperfect self as the mother or not!

'This isn't going to work,' she said, speaking her feelings out loud.

Lewis's eyes narrowed on her. 'What isn't going to work?'

'You,' she said wearily. 'And me....'

'Why ever not? Good God, don't let anything Dinah said spoil things between us. She's an accomplished liar and an expert twister of the truth. What else did she say to you to make you feel like this?'

Olivia struggled to encapsulate the many things Dinah had said. 'She said you selected her as your wife like one would a brood mare, simply because she was young and beautiful and bright. She said you got rid of her when she refused to have your perfect offspring on cue.'

His laugh was bitter. 'What a splendid defence lawyer she would have made!'

'Do you agree you decided to divorce her because she wouldn't stop work and have a baby?'

'It isn't as simple as that, Olivia. I...'

'Please just say yes or no.'

His hands dropped from her shoulders, and his eyes searched hers. 'What is this? Some kind of trial?'

'I need to know the truth,' Olivia insisted.

'Dinah knew what I wanted when I married her. She said she wanted the same things. But she didn't. She lied.'

'Maybe she did, Lewis. Maybe she felt she had to, because she loved you so much. You might not know this, Lewis,' she said, her heart catching, 'but what a woman wants most of all…is to be loved.'

'Not all women, Olivia,' he returned harshly. 'That's a romantic ideal, not reality.'

'It's *my* reality, Lewis. Which is why I know it's not going to work out between us.'

'You won't even give us a chance?'

'No, Lewis. I can't.'

'Why can't you?' he challenged angrily. 'Hell, Olivia, what we shared last night was very special. You think that kind of chemistry happens all the time between couples? You can't throw something like that away just because you imagine you're still in love with Nicholas.'

'That's not it.'

'Then what is it? Tell me one good reason why you and I can't continue to be lovers.'

Fury ignited along her veins. *Sex!* Was that all he wanted from her? Was that all he ever wanted from any woman whom he didn't rate as a perfect ten?

'Very well,' she bit out. 'I'll give you one very good reason. Soon, you won't *want* me as your lover. Soon, that wonderful chemistry you spoke of will fail to spark, because I'll be too big and fat to inspire much in you except revulsion. Yes, Lewis, I see the penny's beginning to drop. Yes, that's right. I'm going to have a baby!'

CHAPTER ELEVEN

EVEN before Lewis's mouth dropped open in shock, Olivia was regretting her hasty words. It was insane to tell him at this stage. She had everything to lose and nothing to gain. Dear God, she would have liked to cut her silly tongue out!

'Does Nicholas know?' he asked in stunned tones.

Olivia stood there for a few seconds, utterly speechless herself. She supposed it was not an illogical conclusion for Lewis to jump to, but she simply hadn't anticipated it.

'No,' she said a bit blankly.

'Are you going to tell him?'

'No,' she repeated, and wondered how long it would take Lewis to reason that Nicholas might not be the father of her baby. 'He wouldn't be interested.'

Lewis's look was contemptuous. 'Good God, what kind of man *is* he? He should be made to face up to his responsibilities. At least give you financial support!'

Olivia found a moment's chilly amusement in his heated condemnation of the man he supposed was the father of her baby. She wondered if he'd be saying that if she pronounced *him* the father. It was easy to be indignant about someone else's bad behaviour.

'I don't want Nicholas to have anything to do with my baby,' she said coldly. 'A baby needs love, Lewis.

A father who doesn't love his child is no use to me.'

And wasn't *that* the truth!

'You're really going to *have* this baby?'

His surprise infuriated her. 'Of course I'm going to have *my* baby!' she shot back at him. 'What did you think?'

'Frankly, I don't think I'm thinking too clearly at the moment.' He raked both hands through his hair. 'You've thrown me for a loop.'

'I'm sure you'll recover shortly.'

He seemed too distracted to appreciate her sarcasm. When he reached out to curl his hands over her shoulders, she stiffened. When his eyes turned soft upon her as well, she had to struggle to keep her emotional distance.

'Have you been to see a doctor yet?' he asked softly.

'I saw my mother's GP over Christmas.'

'Does *she* know? Your mother, I mean.'

'Naturally. I wouldn't keep something like that from my mother.'

'And what did she say? Does she think you should tell Nicholas?'

'No. She thinks he's a creep.'

He nodded. 'A woman of rare judgement. Any man who could…'

His hands suddenly slipped off her shoulders, and he shot her a troubled look. 'Did you know you were pregnant the day of the Christmas party?'

Olivia's stomach flipped right over. He'd finally had second thoughts. The temptation to keep the deception going was acute, but it wasn't right. He had to know. Eventually. He'd never forgive her if she played him for a fool.

'No,' she admitted tautly. 'I didn't.'

His frown deepened. 'But you said you were on the pill…'

'I was. It seems the pill is not always infallible.'

'It was bloody foolproof with Dinah,' he muttered, then frowned at her some more. 'But you said Nicholas had been using condoms as well. To have both methods fail is more than bad luck. It's highly un…'

His voice faltered, and his face went quite ashen. Olivia watched as his logical brain put two and two together and came up with the right answer this time.

'My God, Olivia,' he rasped. 'Are you saying what I think you're saying?'

'You're an intelligent man, Lewis. I'm surprised it took you so long to work it out.'

'There's no doubt in your mind?'

'None at all.' She'd had a period after Nicholas left her. 'If you must blame anyone, blame the caterers at the Christmas party. I had a bout of food poisoning all night after you dropped me off home. It seems gastric upsets can render the pill ineffective.'

She watched him struggle for composure but nothing could hide the fact that he was terribly shaken by the news. Her dismay was overwhelming.

'Why didn't you tell me before this?' he said.

The reproach in his voice sparked a justifiable anger.

'Take a good look at yourself in the mirror, Lewis, and I think you'll be able to guess why. You look like you've just found out your best friend died. It's easy to criticise someone else, isn't it? Not so easy when it's *you* who has to face a responsibility you don't want, one which you haven't planned on but which is yours all the same! I know what happened that day was mostly my fault, but you were all for accepting half the blame afterwards. It seems that doesn't quite extend to embracing parenthood, especially with an inferior species of woman.'

'Dinah's filled your head with rubbish,' he snapped. 'I don't think you're inferior at all. In fact, you make ten of Dinah.'

'Around the butt, maybe. But not in any other way. I know what I look like, Lewis. I'm passably pretty when I'm made up. My skin's good and my figure's not bad when I keep off the chocolates. But I'm ordinary fare compared to Dinah. I'm sure that, given a choice, I would not be on your short list for the privilege of producing your perfect offspring.'

'For pity's sake, I never wanted my offspring to be perfect! I never said any such thing to Dinah. Okay, so one day, early in our marriage, I made some idle remark about how we were sure to have good-looking children. Do you honestly think I really care about something as superficial as that?'

'I don't know, Lewis. Do you?'

'Believe me, all I care about is having healthy children.'

'I'd like to believe you. But I'll wait and see for myself, thank you very much. Meanwhile, you're looking a little shell-shocked, Lewis. But I can appreciate that. I've cruelled all your plans, haven't I?

There again, having the boss's baby is not exactly what *I* planned, either. But not to worry; I don't expect anything from you. I don't expect anything from any man any more. Now I want to go home, thank you very much.'

Heart racing and head pounding, she brushed past him and stomped down the remaining stairs. But when she stepped onto the marble floor her right foot landed on a big bit of violet glass and her leg began to shoot out from under her.

Her cry carried true panic as the most horrible scenario flashed before her eyes: her crashing heavily to the rock-hard floor; pain jarring through her whole pelvis; her tiny baby being dislodged from the warm sanctuary of her womb.

When Lewis's saving hands scooped under her arms and stopped her fall, she was sick with relief. When he turned her round and gathered her close, she sagged, sobbing, into the warm security of his solid male frame. 'Oh, Lewis,' she cried. 'I thought...for a moment...I was so afraid...for the baby.'

'For *our* baby,' he corrected her as he clasped her tight. 'I know,' he continued, his voice actually shaking. 'Me too. I've never moved so fast in all my life.'

Taken aback by the emotion in his voice, she drew back and glanced up at him, surprise in her eyes. 'You really *want* this baby?'

'I didn't realise how much till I saw you falling.'

Olivia felt torn by his admission. As much as she was touched by his wanting their baby, she wanted him to want *her* as well. Not just in bed, or in a shower or across a desk, but in his heart and in his life, for ever and ever. She wanted him to love her with a love which would never die, because once she had his baby she knew that was what her love for him would be like.

'We'll have to get married,' he said. 'As soon as my divorce comes through.'

Olivia sucked in a startled breath, her shocked delight taking some time to give way to the unromantic reality of his proposal. She would not have been human if she still wasn't tempted to go along with such a marriage. Her mother would think she was crazy to refuse Lewis's offer.

But she wasn't her mother. She had to be true to herself. And to her dreams.

'That's very kind of you, Lewis,' she said with true regret in her voice. 'Very kind. But I don't believe in marrying for anything other than love.'

His blue eyes grew steely, as they did when things didn't go right for him at work. When they started glittering with an even harder light, Olivia knew she'd been moved into the category of a very difficult problem, one which had to be solved at all costs.

'Very well, Olivia,' he said, his teeth clenched in his jaw. 'I suppose I'll have to accept that answer for now. But the matter's not concluded. I aim to ask again. And I aim to get a different answer next time.'

No doubt he *would* ask again. Lewis was a stubborn man. And no doubt she would struggle to keep on saying no. But she had no intention of saying yes till he declared his undying love for her, and she actually believed him.

Words would not be enough. She would have to see his love in action.

And she wasn't talking about sex! There would be no more of that. No more fulfilling his little fantasies, either at work or at the weekends. No doubt Lewis thought he could get around her that way, by using the chemistry he spoke of to undermine her resolve not to surrender to his will. She'd been very weak where he was concerned last night.

But no more! She would keep him at a safe distance in future.

The realisation that she was standing within the confines of his embrace at that very moment brought another debilitating wave of weakness. It *did* feel good in his arms. *Too* good.

'Would you drive me home now, please?' she asked stiffly while trying to disentangle herself from his arms.

She succeeded in removing them from around her back but he merely took hold of her by the shoulders instead.

'There's no need to go home,' he said soothingly, bedroom blue eyes raking over her face and figure. 'Stay. I'll cook you some breakfast. We can talk some more.'

Make love some more, more likely!

She flushed at the thought. 'Not now, Lewis,' she said firmly. 'I have things I have to do at home today.'

'When can I see you, then? Tonight?' he suggested, smiling ever so sweetly down at her. 'I'll take you out to dinner. Somewhere special. We can celebrate the baby together.'

Olivia sighed. Already she could see his battle plan to win her over. Corrupt her with his money and seduce her with his charm. It would be a difficult combination to resist, especially when he'd already won her heart.

But he didn't know that, did he?

'I don't think so, Lewis.'

'Why not?'

She could hardly say she was refusing because she was afraid to be alone with him like that till she'd marshalled some more defences against him. Last night was too fresh in her mind. It would be so easy to give in to him once more, to lose herself in the mindless pleasures he was capable of evoking in her weak female flesh.

'Can't a girl just say no to you?'

'You're not any girl,' he suddenly snapped. 'You're the mother of my child.'

Ah. She did so like it when he laid out his priorities so clearly. Now she knew where she stood. It seemed her role as mother of his baby had taken over from her more recent role of sex-goddess secretary.

'So I am,' she said. 'Something I've known for a little longer than you, Lewis. I suggest you spend the rest of the weekend thinking about what that entails and we'll talk again on Monday.'

'I won't have changed my mind,' he growled.

'About what?'

'About our getting married.'

'And neither will I, Lewis.'

He looked at her as though she'd grown three heads. 'You do realise that I'm a very wealthy man,' he said with a measure of disbelief in his voice. 'As my wife, you could have anything you want.'

Oh, no, I couldn't, she thought, and her heart turned over. Because what I really want is the one thing you're incapable of giving me!

'How nice,' she murmured. 'Can we go now?'

He didn't speak a word to her on the drive home. The car fairly vibrated with his fury and frustration. Olivia had never seen him this angry before, not even when he had that trouble with the advertising agency. His knuckles were white on the steering wheel and he kept pursing and unpursing his lips. By the time he pulled in outside her block of flats, you could almost see the air pulsating around his mouth.

'So tell me,' he bit out as he cast a disapproving eye over the ancient building which housed her flat. 'If for some weird and wonderful reason you refuse my next offer of marriage, is this where you intend to raise my child?'

'No. I have sufficient savings to put a deposit on a nice little unit somewhere. Not a fancy suburb, of course. It'll have to be in the Western suburbs. But there again, I guess I'm a Western suburbs type of person. Working class and down to earth.'

'Hmmph! And what about after the baby is born? I suppose you'll put it in child care practically before its eyes are open.'

'It'll be a baby, Lewis, not a kitten. His or her eyes will be open from birth. And no, I have no intention of putting my baby in child care. I hope to set myself up in a secretarial and word processing business which will enable me to look after my baby at home.

Since you've told me how wealthy you are, maybe you, as the father, might buy me some computer equipment to help out.'

'Great. I get to buy computer equipment. Just what a father's always needed for! What about the nursery? And all the other things a baby will need? I've heard that can run into thousands!'

'Only if you buy everything new. I'm a dab hand at doing up second-hand furniture. And I sew extremely well. I don't believe in wasting money.'

'Good God, Olivia, you said you were cheap, but this is cheap to end all cheaps! My child is not going to be wheeled around in some rusty old second-hand pram. Neither will it sleep where God knows who or what has slept before!'

Olivia was both amused and heartened by his passion. At least he was capable of that. She smiled at his flushed face and furious eyes. 'You're a snob, Lewis, do you know that?'

'My mother *has* accused me of that vice.'

'A woman of rare judgement.'

'You have a sharp wit, madam, and a tongue to match.'

'One out of two ain't bad, then,' she countered drily.

'What on earth are you talking about?'

'Not beautiful,' she said ruefully, 'but bright.'

His exasperation amused Olivia no end.

'I'm going to strangle Dinah when I next see her, which will be very shortly. I aim on auctioning that bloody house as quickly as possible so that I can get her off my back and out of my life.'

'Poor Dinah.'

'Poor Dinah, my foot. She won't be damned poor once she gets her divorce settlement. Still, I dare say she'll think it was just payment for two years married to a fool.'

Olivia's heart softened. 'Oh, Lewis,' she said gently, 'you're far from being a fool. But you shouldn't have married her if you didn't really love her.'

He sighed. 'Maybe you're right. But what is real love, Olivia? Are you so sure you know?'

'Oh, yes,' she nodded, looking straight at him. 'I know...'

'Then I envy you.'

'Don't. It hurts when it's not returned.'

'You'll get over him, Olivia,' he said irritably. 'Trust me.'

She kept silent at this and he sighed anew. 'I suppose you're not going to let me come up with you.'

'No.'

'You're very strong-willed, aren't you?'

She had to laugh. 'In some things, but not in others.'

He leant over and kissed her firmly on the lips. Her head jerked back against the seat, which wasn't such a good idea because it left her nowhere to go. He merely leaned over further and kissed her all the harder. Her earlier vow to keep him at a safe distance could not compete with the hunger in his kiss. If nothing else, she supposed he did want this from her. With a soft moan of defeat, her lips parted to accept the invasion of his tongue.

It was one of the longest, most impassioned kisses she had ever experienced, stripping her of all pretence and promising nothing but sexual submission from her whenever he wanted.

And he seemed to sense it.

'Dare I hope this is one area where you're not too strong-willed?' he murmured against her totally melted mouth.

'I...I do seem to have a weakness when it comes to the pleasures of the flesh.'

His head lifted far enough for him to look deep into her dark, dilated eyes. 'That's not what Nicholas accused you of before he left you. He called you boring in bed, if I recall. Believe me when I tell you I don't find you boring *in* bed, or out of it.'

She coloured fiercely. 'You...you seem to have tapped into a side of myself previously unexplored.'

'Mmm. I like the sound of that,' he said, and glanced down at the rapid rise and fall of her breasts.

'Don't,' she said, suddenly afraid of what he might do.

He settled back in his seat and slanted her a rueful look. 'Might I remind you that your good reason for our not continuing as lovers no longer exists, Olivia? I don't find the idea of making love to you in the coming months even remotely repulsive. Unless the doctor says it's dangerous, I see no reason why we should deny ourselves the comfort and pleasure of each other's bodies.'

Olivia could only admire the smoothness of his spiel. Still, his brutally seductive kiss proved it was probably better she agree up front to continue their physical relationship rather than say no to his face, then a reluctant yes whenever he took her in his arms. That was hardly the way to his respecting her as a person.

But she had to make limits, or lose respect for herself.

'You're probably right,' she said matter-of-factly. 'I do recognise the chemistry between us. But I *would* like to see the doctor first and make sure sex is okay. Even if I'm given the go-ahead, I must insist that you refrain from any advances in the office.'

'God, Olivia, you sound like you're conducting a business deal.'

'Sorry. I guess I'm not used to this sort of thing.'

'And you think I am?'

'I don't know. I've only known you just over eighteen months. I have no idea what you got up to before then.'

'Nothing quite like this, I assure you,' he bit out. 'All right. Nothing doing till you've seen the doctor, and no hanky panky around the office. Am I to be restricted over what I buy you and the baby as well?'

'I can hardly stop you buying the baby things, but leave me out of the present-buying, please. I would look upon any personal gifts as bribery and corruption.'

'Good grief! I can't believe this. What about my mother?' he flung at her.

'What about her?'

'Can I tell her the good news?'

'Will she think it's good news?'

'You'd better believe it! She's been wanting to be

a grandmother for the last ten years. She's going to descend upon you like a plague of locusts. As for present-buying…Momma darling is going to make me look like a cheapskate by comparison!'

'She sounds wonderful,' Olivia said warmly.

'She is,' Lewis agreed. 'She's also going to want to meet you.'

'That's all right. I want to meet her too. Just not this weekend, please, Lewis.'

'If you insist.'

'I insist. Now I must go. Thank you for driving me home.'

'Must you be so formal?'

'Yes.'

'Why?'

'Because…' She was out of the car before he could grab her and kiss her again. 'See you Monday morning,' she mouthed through the window before hurrying off.

She heard the telephone ringing as she came up the stairs. She ran, but thought it would have stopped by the time she got inside. It hadn't, however, the sound insistent and persistent. Whoever it was was determined to reach her. Frowning, Olivia hurried across her small living room and swept up the receiver.

CHAPTER TWELVE

'YES?' she said breathlessly.

'It's Mum, Olivia. Goodness, you sound like you've been running.'

'I have been.'

'Where have you been? I tried to get you last night but there was no answer. And this is the third time I've called this morning.'

'Oh?' Olivia decided not to try to explain. 'What's wrong?'

'Nothing's wrong. In fact, the news is very good. That's why I was so anxious to tell you. Your father's got a job. A really good one.'

'But that's marvellous!' Olivia exclaimed before suddenly remembering Lewis had said he'd see what he could do for her father. 'What kind of job?' she asked, wondering if this was a coincidence. After all, Lewis hadn't said anything to her last night.

'You'd never guess in a million years,' her mother said excitedly.

'No. No, I don't think I would. Just tell me.'

'Well, it's a type of caretaker job on a property up this way which agists racehorses. Mostly mares in foal, as well as some racing horses out on spells. All your father has to do is feed and water them, and call the vet if anything looks wrong.'

'That's great, Mum. Um…how…how did Dad hear of this job?'

'It was the strangest thing. The owners rang the local employment office and asked specifically for him. They'd heard from a friend of a friend that he was a very good worker, honest and reliable. All they needed to know was if he knew anything about horses. They were absolutely thrilled when he went out to the property for an interview and showed them how much he *did* know. Being a country-reared boy, there's nothing Dave doesn't know about horses. And of course he's such a capable man with his hands. You've no idea the change in him when he came home and said he'd got the job. He's going round all puffed up like a peacock.'

Olivia was astonished to find herself close to tears. Pregnant women were supposed to be emotional, but this was ridiculous! She should be grinning from ear to ear. Instead, she felt awfully fragile all of a sudden.

'I'm…I'm so pleased for him,' she choked out, unbearably moved that Lewis would bother to follow through with his offer. It had to be Lewis's doing, of course. Why else would anyone specifically ask for her father? The fact that he'd done this for her family *before* he knew about the baby meant a lot to her. It showed him to be a genuine and generous-hearted man.

'We're moving in tomorrow,' her mother was rattling on. 'Oh, Olivia, you should see the house. It's so huge, with the loveliest big old kitchen. The outside's a bit run-down. But nothing that Dave can't fix. He asked if he could work on it a bit in his spare time and they said that would be wonderful. They offered to pay for any materials he had to buy and throw in a bonus after the work was done. So what do you think of that?'

'I…I think it's the best news I've heard for a long time,' she said, tears running down her face.

'Are you all right, Olivia?' her mother asked sharply. 'You sound odd. You're not crying, are you?'

Olivia sniffled. 'Just a little bit.'

'I have to confess I had a weep when I first heard, and then again when I saw the house. I've never had a house with four bedrooms before. And there's this lovely little sewing room off the back verandah.'

'You both deserve a change of luck, Mum.'

'Your father certainly does. He's a good man, Olivia, and he's always done the best he could. It wasn't easy for him having to get married when he was only a boy himself.'

'I understand that, Mum. Truly.'

'I hope so. And, speaking of having to get married, that doesn't mean it wouldn't work out splendidly in your case. Your boss is a man, not a boy, with plenty to offer a wife and child.'

'That's what *he* said.'

'Good Lord, you've told him?'

'Yes. Just this morning.'

'And he wants to marry you?'

'Yes.'

'Thank heavens be praised!'

Olivia winced at having to tell her elated mother the truth. 'Mum…please don't get carried away. I…er…I said no.'

'You said *what*?'

Olivia winced again.

'Good God, what's wrong with you, girl? Have you lost your marbles?'

'Well, I...I...'

'Pride!' her mother pronounced irritably. 'You've always had too much pride. He might not ask you again, do you realise that?'

'He...he said he would.' Olivia sighed at her suddenly quavering voice. Why was it mothers could always make you become defensive and doubtful, even when the decisions you'd made had felt right at the time?

'Did he, now?' her mother said, sounding slightly mollified and extremely curious. 'Well, I suppose that's a positive sign. So what was his reaction when you first told him?'

Olivia swallowed to clear the ongoing thickness in her throat. 'I think, after the initial shock, he was quite pleased. It seems his marriage broke up because his wife refused to stop work and have children.'

'Stupid woman! But her selfishness is your gain, Olivia. If you play your cards right, you'll have everything you ever wanted. And you'll be able to give your children all the advantages you never had.'

Olivia sighed. 'You know, Mum, I'm not so sure I had that right.'

'Had what right, dear?'

'The importance of money. I think I underestimated what you and Dad gave us girls when we were growing up. I'm beginning to think love and encouragement and acceptance are far more important parental gifts than material things. We always had plenty of love and approval from both of you.'

'Oh, Olivia...what a sweet thing to say. You've no idea how much that means to me as a mother. I...I always felt that I'd let you down, that I'd been selfish in keeping you, then in having more babies.'

'Don't ever think that, Mum. Never! You did the right thing. You've been a wonderful mother. I only hope I can be as wonderful a mother when my turn comes.'

'It's a hard job to do alone, Olivia.'

'Yes; yes, I can appreciate that.' But it was also a hard job to do if you were unhappy. Better she and Lewis stay unmarried and good friends than married and fighting all the time. Because people did fight when one loved and the other didn't. She'd seen such marriages lots of times. They usually ended up in divorce, with emotionally destroyed parents and children.

'If and when Lewis asks you again,' her mother said with a soft sigh, 'promise me you'll give it a lot of serious thought.'

'I will, Mum. I promise.'

'Good girl. Now I must be off. Your father's taking me to the movies today as a celebration. You know, it's been over two years since I've been to the movies. I have no idea what we're going to see. Frankly, I don't much care. I'll enjoy it whatever it is. Bye now, love. And look after yourself.'

'Bye, Mum...'

Olivia hung up slowly, her promise to her mother weighing heavily on her mind. She hoped Lewis didn't ask her again too soon. Because she could not in all conscience say yes, simply for security. She'd meant it when she'd told her mother she no longer thought money was the be-all and end-all she'd once imagined.

On the other hand, it was going to be hard to keep on saying no when everyone else wanted her to say yes. No doubt Lewis's mother would join forces with her own mother, and push for the parents-to-be to wed. People of their generation could not conceive of any other solution. It was the done thing.

But it wasn't the done thing any more!

Olivia had to keep reminding herself of that, as well as the reason she'd said no. Lewis didn't love her. She simply could not live as his wife with that knowledge. It would make her emotionally insecure. And being emotionally insecure was much worse than being financially insecure. Much, much worse!

No, she'd done the right thing, she decided as she walked into her small kitchen and set about making some toast for her hunger-panged stomach.

Olivia believed in doing the right thing, which was why her conscience started troubling her over breakfast. She really should ring Lewis and thank him for getting her father that job. No matter what his motives, it had been a thoughtful thing to do.

She didn't want to ring. She didn't want to have any further contact with Lewis over the coming weekend. She really needed to bury her head in the sand for a couple of days and pretend she wasn't even pregnant. She needed to do mindless things like washing and cleaning and ironing. She needed some space.

Smiling wryly to herself at this last thought, she decided to get the unfortunate phone call over as quickly as possible.

Lewis answered on the second ring.

'Yes?' he snapped.

'It's Olivia, Lewis.'

'Yes?'

'I…I just wanted to ring and say thank you for getting my father a job. He and Mum are both thrilled to pieces.'

'And you, Olivia?' he asked drily. 'Are you thrilled to pieces?'

'I'm very grateful.'

'*How* grateful?' he said, a dark mockery flavouring the words.

Everything inside Olivia tightened. This was why she hadn't wanted to make the call. She'd known, instinctively, that Lewis would try to use her gratitude against her. Her boss was never at his best when things weren't going his way.

'Not *that* grateful,' she countered.

'As they don't say in the classics, Olivia, Monday is another day.' And he hung up.

CHAPTER THIRTEEN

COME Monday morning, Olivia was already sitting at her desk, her prim white blouse buttoned up to the neck, when Lewis swept in right on eight-thirty, wearing a well cut dark blue suit and a wide smile.

'Good morning, Olivia,' he announced on his way through to his office. 'Lovely day, isn't it? No coffee this morning, thank you. I had a late breakfast with my mother. Which reminds me…' He ground to a halt beside her desk. 'Keep lunch free. Mum wants us to join her. Is that all right with you?'

'Er…'

'You might as well get it over with today,' he advised drily. 'It won't get any easier with the passage of time.'

Did anything? Olivia thought wearily. The weekend had dragged interminably, tension mounting within her after Lewis's none too subtle threat. By the time this morning had come, she'd worked herself up into a sick state of nerves. She didn't need morning sickness. Her stomach was managing to swirl crazily all by itself without the help of her maternal hormones.

'All right,' she said with resignation in her voice.

'Sensible girl. There again…' His eyes swept over her. 'You *are* a sensible girl, aren't you? Or you *look* like one, anyway. I'm sure Mother will be very impressed.'

143

He strode on into his office, leaving Olivia feeling very conscious of what Dinah had called her school-marm image. She'd toyed with a new hairstyle this morning. And more make-up. And even a more col-ourful outfit. But had discarded each idea as silly and futile.

Which it probably was.

But she still wished she looked a little softer this morning, and not so severe. She didn't think Lewis's mother would be impressed at all!

'Olivia?'

Her head snapped up to find Lewis standing beside her desk again. He handed her a sheet of paper. 'Here are the names of three Melbourne advertising agencies which were recommended to me over the weekend. Please call them and make appointments for us to visit them on next Wednesday afternoon, Thursday morn-ing and Thursday afternoon. We'll fly down Wednesday morning, *not* during peak hour. Book us a car to meet us at the airport and shuttle us around for those two days. Book us a room at a decent hotel in the city for the Wednesday. It doesn't matter which. We'll fly back Thursday evening.'

Olivia had to work hard to stop her mouth from flapping open like a fish. 'You...you said book *us* a room,' she croaked out. 'Do you mean...only one room...between the two of us?'

'Yes, of course.'

'Of course,' she repeated dazedly, and he smiled a slow, smug smile.

'So glad you agree with me. Why go to the unnec-essary and wasted expense of two rooms when we'll be sharing the bed? You agreed to continue our affair, Olivia. And Melbourne is not the office.'

'I...I know.' She could hardly think. Her mind was already in that hotel room, in bed with him. *Already.*

She wanted to slap his smoothly sexy face; wanted to hate him for doing this to her.

But she couldn't. She loved him and she wanted him. She wanted him so much, all of a sudden it was as if a secret engine had been switched on in her body which was stoking up to a full head of steam and making her feel hot all over.

'By the way, I do realise you're a stickler for budgets, but I have an aversion to sitting next to strangers when I'm cooped up in a plane. So business class, please. You too, of course,' he went on with the silky arrogance of the very handsome and very rich. 'Right next to me. Can't have my personal assistant being chatted up by some sleazy salesman on the make, can I?'

He was gone again, leaving her flushed and flustered. She now regretted thanking him for getting her father that job. He probably *had* only done so as a seductive ploy, not because he was such a good guy.

Good guys didn't coerce and corrupt, which was exactly what this Melbourne trip was about. Those advertising agencies would have come to him for the All Woman account. Heck, they'd have flown right round Australia and kissed Lewis's feet, if that was what he'd wanted!

But no, he had to go to them. Why? Because he wanted her alone, alone and out of her usual environment. He wanted her in a luxurious hotel room in a huge downy bed with expensive sheets and a million-dollar view. He wanted her wined and dined and totally without will, seduced and reduced to nothing but his mindless love slave.

Olivia shuddered at the perverse pleasure her thoughts automatically evoked.

Naturally, she knew that the sex was only a means to an end for Lewis. He wasn't dying to make love to her again. The way he'd just looked her over had hardly betrayed uncontrollable passion. He meant to ask her to marry him once more when she was trembling beneath him, when her mind was mush and she would do almost anything he asked of her.

She shuddered again in silent admission of her weakness in this regard.

What would she say this time? she agonised. Would she have the strength to refuse him a second time? Would she be even *capable* of saying no?

Olivia jumped to her feet, unable to sit there quietly any longer. She felt hopelessly confused and hopelessly aroused.

Her eyes flung daggers at his closed office door. What a wicked devil he was. A devious and wicked devil!

'No!' she shouted at the door. 'The answer will still be *no*!'

The door was flung open and Olivia felt really stupid, standing there with her red face and heaving breasts.

Lewis wasn't at all red-faced or heaving. He looked elegant and sophisticated and superbly in control.

'Did you call out, Olivia?' he asked coolly.

She clenched her fists and gritted her teeth. 'I said no,' she bit out.

His expression was the epitome of classic urbane composure. 'No? No what?'

'No to marrying you!'

His eyebrows lifted. 'But Olivia...I haven't asked you again yet. Please give me the courtesy of waiting till I do.' And he shut the door again.

She glared at the door and almost stamped her feet, she was so mad. Whirling, she strode from her office and down the corridor to the ladies' room. There, she stayed in one of the cubicles for much longer than necessary, calming herself and regaining some much needed control over her emotions.

When she emerged, one of the secretaries from Marketing, who always looked a million dollars, was titivating herself in front of the mirror. She had very short, very blonde hair, and was wearing a snazzy little cream crêpe suit. As she leant forward to reapply her lipstick, her trendily cropped jacket hung open, revealing a body-hugging red vest with a low V neckline. In front of her, on the vanity bench, sat a make-up purse brimful of every conceivable item of cosmetic help.

Olivia had a sudden thought. 'Lila...' she began as she moved alongside and started washing her hands.

Lila turned and smiled with her perfectly outlined lips. 'Yes?' They knew each other to speak to, but had never socialised.

'I wonder if I might ask a favour of you?' Olivia went on. 'My boss has sprung this special business lunch on me and I'm not really dressed for the part today. I need some sprucing up. Do you think I might borrow a bit of your make-up?'

'Oh, sure! What would you like?'

'What do you think? You always look so fantastic.'

'Gee, that's sweet of you to say so, Olivia. If you like, I could do your face for you.'

'Would you?'

'I'd love to. Makeovers are my speciality. Look at me. My own mother hardly recognises me these days.'

Olivia had to smile. No doubt she'd had better base material to work with than in her case. 'I don't want a complete makeover. Just a touch here and there.'

'It's amazing what a touch here and there can do, especially when you have big brown eyes and such beautiful bones.'

Olivia was startled. 'Me? Beautiful bones?'

'You mean you hadn't noticed?'

'Well, I know I have nice eyes...'

'Believe me, your bones are better. And I would *kill* for your hair. Mine was the colour of a faded fence before I decided to hit the blonding creme, whereas yours looks like polished mahogany. And I just love the way you slick it back from your face. That's very in, you know. And kinda sexy. I've always thought that if you just showed a bit more of your figure and highlighted the good points in your face you'd have all the men around here drooling.'

'Really?'

'Trust me.'

'I tell you what, Lila. Could we postpone the makeover till morning tea? Then you can give me the works.'

'My pleasure. What's the special occasion, by the way?'

'Let's just say I want a certain someone to sit up and take some extra notice of me.' And I'd like him to be as uncomfortable as he made me this morning! she added silently. By the time Thursday night comes, I want him to have forgotten all about marriage and think of nothing but the moment!

'Oooh.' Lila pursed her pretty glossed mouth and rolled her long-lashed eyes. 'I take it the rumours about you and the boss are spot-on for once?'

Olivia contemplated lying, then decided why bother? In time, all the staff at Altman Industries were going to see for themselves exactly what had been going on between the boss and his secretary.

'Let's just say there's been a slight shift in our relationship,' she said with a poker face.

Lila grinned. 'But you'd like to shift it some more. Wow! This is going to be fun. But make-up isn't going to be enough, Olivia. You need to do something about that blouse of yours. I know some men have schoolgirl fetishes but I honestly don't think Mr Altman's that kind of guy. Not if that glamour-puss wife of his was anything to go by! How about you wear my red top? I can always do up my jacket for a couple of hours.'

Olivia sucked in a sharp breath. Dared she?

She thought of Mrs Altman taking one look at her as she was and thinking she was some mousy little amenable thing who could be pushed around. Then she thought of the smugly superior expression which had swept across Lewis's face as he'd looked her over this morning.

Did she dare change her image that much? Too damned right she did!

CHAPTER FOURTEEN

'Wow!' Lila exclaimed once the transformation was complete. She stepped back to view Olivia from head to toe, but frowned when she came to the sensible black pumps.

'They spoil everything,' she said. 'You need height to show off those great legs of yours. What size shoe do you take?'

'Seven and a half.'

'Wait here. I'll be back shortly.'

Olivia waited nervously, almost afraid to look at herself. She looked so different. So...striking.

Full eye make-up had made her brown eyes look enormous, and her scarlet mouth demanded to be noticed. But it was the scarlet top which worried Olivia the most. On Lila's neat little figure it had looked startling enough. On her own more voluptuous curves, it was decidedly provocative.

Lila swept back into the ladies' room, waving a pair of black patent stilettos. 'Courtesy of one of our fellow secretaries!'

'This has been really great of you, Lila,' Olivia said as she kicked off her shoes. 'Thank you so much. And thank whoever belongs to these shoes. I'll look after them. And I'll try not to spill anything on your top.'

'Don't be silly. It's wash and wear.' And she flashed Olivia a lovely smile. It made Olivia regret that she'd never bothered to be more friendly with the girls in the office before. They were much nicer than she'd realised.

But better late than never, she decided, and smiled warmly back.

'Well, what do you think?' she said, glancing down at her sexily shod feet.

'Turn over the waistband of your skirt,' Lila advised.

She did and it hitched the hemline higher, showing more thigh than she'd ever shown before in the office.

Lila grinned and made a circle with her thumb and forefinger. 'Perfect! Now you'll knock him dead.'

'Oh, I don't want him dead,' Olivia countered saucily. 'I want him very much alive.'

Lila laughed. 'I didn't realise you were such a wag.'

'Neither did I!' Olivia said. And they both laughed.

'Now give me your shoes. I'll hide them under my desk till you get back. That way, you'll have to come and get them, and then I can hear how things went.'

It was five to twelve by the time Olivia left the ladies' room. Lewis had told her around ten that morning to be ready by twelve, and whilst she would have liked to be fashionably late she couldn't quite summon that kind of courage. Or rudeness. She wanted to impress Lewis's mother with her style and assurance, not get on her wrong side by being late.

As she hurried back down the corridor towards her office, one of the male clerks in Accounts passed her by, and his head nearly swivelled off his shoulders as he gawked at her new look.

A small smile of satisfaction was playing on Olivia's glossed lips as she walked through her open office door, though the sight of Lewis glaring at her from *his* open doorway almost wiped it from her face for a moment. Till she saw his expressive blue eyes glittering wildly as they raked over her plunging neckline.

'Good God, what have you done to yourself?' he exclaimed a mite thickly.

'Just spruced myself up a bit,' she returned airily, and continued over to her desk, picking up her handbag and dropping the scarlet lipstick inside. Lila had said she might need a touch-up after lunch. 'Can't have your mum thinking you've got yourself involved with some dowdy little piece from hicksville.'

For once in his life, he was speechless, though only for several seconds. 'What sort of game are you playing at, Olivia?' he demanded to know.

Her eyes snapped up, flashing angrily at him. 'I never play games, Lewis. I leave that to the men in this world. I'm straight as a die and honest as the day is long. And don't you ever forget it!'

Her heart raced as her hands found her hips. 'Might I remind you that I adopted my drab image in this office in deference to Dinah's feelings. It came to me this morning that dressing down had become a bad habit. People sometimes mistake the outside for the inside. I don't like people underestimating me,' she finished, and held his eyes boldly.

'I would never do that.'

'I hope not.'

His smile unnerved her. 'Shall we go, then?' he

said coolly, his momentary lapse in composure well
and truly over. 'It's gone twelve.'

'That's your fault for making a fuss. I was here on
time.'

'I know,' he said, and took her arm. 'That's one of
the many things I like about you. Your reliability.'

Five minutes later, they were stopped at a set of
red lights on Victoria Road and an awkward silence
fell between them. Olivia was sitting there stiffly with
her handbag in her lap when, out of the corner of her
eye, she saw Lewis give her a long, assessing look.

'You look good,' he said. '*Too* good,' he added
drily.

Her head snapped round, her scarlet lips parting
with surprise. 'How…how can you look *too* good?'

'You made me promise not to touch you around
the office. If this is what I'm going to have to look
forward to from now on, things could get a
mite…strained.'

'Oh.' How strange, she thought. One of the reasons
she'd allowed Lila to make her over was that she'd
wanted to make Lewis as uncomfortable as he'd made
her this morning. The reality of his telling her he was
just that now brought feelings of guilt and shame. She
knew male frustration was far more acute and painful
than a woman's. To deliberately torment him *was* a
type of game-playing, a cruel and malicious game.

'I'm sorry, Lewis. I…I didn't think.'

'You have no reason to be sorry,' he said. 'You
have the right to wear whatever you like. In truth,
you're not dressed nearly as provocatively as my previous secretary. The funny thing is she never so much

as raised a trickle of sweat in me, whereas you, Olivia... God knows, I don't seem to be able to control myself at all where you're concerned these days. Things were bad enough when you came to work looking as prim and pure as a nun. Fact is I was beginning to think that was why I was wanting you so much. I imagined it was a kind of reverse psychology. The cooler you looked, the hotter my thoughts. But now I see I was fooling myself in that regard. My thoughts are much hotter at this moment.'

No hotter than her own. 'Lewis,' she choked out, her cheeks flaming. 'Please don't keep talking about this.'

He slanted her a searing look, and said in the softest, sexiest voice, 'Come home with me tonight.'

Olivia bit her bottom lip and battled with temptation, till she remembered her doctor's appointment at eight o'clock.

It was exactly what she needed to get her mind—and her wayward body—back on track. She was having a baby. That was her first and only priority.

'I can't, Lewis,' she said firmly. 'I have a doctor's appointment. Please stop making life difficult for me.'

'*Me*, stop making life difficult for *you*?'

The light turned green at that moment, and Lewis fumed silently for a few seconds while he accelerated away. But his outburst had only been delayed, and he was soon on the rampage again.

'Do you have any idea how difficult you've made my life since the day you decided to get plastered and show yours truly just how damned sexy you could be? I spent a bloody awful Christmas worried sick that you were off somewhere taking an overdose of sleeping tablets. Any feelings of relief at your safe return to work were soon expelled by a raging desire to have you show me how sexy you were again in every position of the Kama Sutra!'

Olivia's eyes grew wider and wider upon him with each successive revelation.

'And then,' he ground out, 'then, when I thought I would at least be able to get some peace by our becoming lovers, you drop the bombshell that the pill failed back before Christmas and you're having my baby! Crown that off with your refusal to marry me—even for the sake of the child!—and I'd say it's you who's making life difficult for me, don't you think?'

She gulped and faced the front again. 'Er…I hadn't really looked at it quite that way before.'

'Huh! Typical woman. Doesn't give a man credit for having any feelings at all!'

'That's not true,' she argued. 'It's just that most men's feelings are rooted below the waist.'

'That's not their fault. Mother Nature made men that way deliberately. If sex wasn't a male priority the human race would have died out centuries ago.'

'And if women weren't nurturers the same would have happened. I'm going to be a mother, Lewis. My baby has to come first with me.'

'And I admire you for that. I really do. But don't forget that I'm going to become a father at the same time you become a mother. In the old days, a father only had to produce, provide and protect his family. But nowadays psychologists are finding out that fathers should be more actively involved in the day-today upbringing of their children. How can I do that from a distance? I need to be there, under the same roof. Or at least very close by.'

'Yes,' she murmured. 'Yes, I can see that.'

'All I ask is for you to think about that the next time I ask you to marry me. Mind you, I'm not asking you again yet. I can see I rushed you. But I will ask you again, Olivia. When I feel the time is right.'

Olivia sighed. Now he'd made her feel guilty for having refused him the first time. Guilty and selfish.

'Here's Mum's block of flats.'

As Lewis slid his navy car into the kerb, Olivia glanced up at the impressively modern building which rose four storeys high into the summer sky. It had pale blue cement-rendered walls, trimmed with white-framed windows and doors. The overall effect was cool and clean and classy.

'It looks fairly new,' Olivia said.

'It's a couple of years old.'

'Does your mum own or rent?'

'She owns the whole building. I built it, then gave it to her before my marriage to Dinah. I wanted her to be financially secure for life, as well as totally independent of me, just in case the business ever went bust or bankrupt.'

Olivia stared up at the building and wondered how many apartments it housed. The rents would command a lot more than her own crummy old building. Even if there were only a dozen flats, the weekly income from them would be formidable. It seemed Mrs Altman had been well rewarded by her son for all her sacrifices over the years.

'That was very generous of you, Lewis,' she said.

'I'm very generous to those I love. And those I want to bribe and corrupt,' he added with a dry little smile. 'Do you think you come into one of those categories?'

He was being facetious, she knew. 'I can't see how I'd qualify for either category,' she countered archly. 'I would never contemplate marrying a man who resorted to bribery and corruption to get what he wanted.'

Or one who didn't love me...

'You don't know what you'd contemplate, Olivia,' Lewis said ruefully, 'until you're faced with the actual situation. These past few weeks have taught me that. Now do stop arguing with me and come along. Mum's as allergic to tardiness as you are. And her name is Betty, by the way. She was named Margaret, but likes to be called Betty.'

Betty Altman looked younger than her photo, and had the same sharp blue eyes as her son. They swept over Olivia with an all-encompassing glance, their expression reflecting a wry amusement.

'I'll have to take Lewis to task over his capacity to adequately describe women,' she said as she ushered Olivia inside, leaving Lewis to trail in after them and shut the door. 'Attractive is far too inadequate a word for you, Olivia. And brunette doesn't do justice to your hair. Now give me a hug and a kiss, my dear. It's not every day I meet the darling girl who's going to give me my first grandchild.

'My, but you *are* a healthy-looking girl!' she added when she finally drew back to look at Olivia some more. 'I'm so sick to death of young women looking like they haven't had a decent meal in weeks. It's a pleasure to see one with good child-bearing hips.'

Olivia laughed. 'I think I have child-bearing boobs to match.'

'And perfectly splendid they are, too,' Betty complimented. 'You're going to breast-feed?'

'I hope to. Mum says it's not only better for the baby, it's cheaper.'

Lewis made some sort of snorting sound from behind them which brought a narrow-eyed glare from his mother. 'And what are *you* objecting to, my lad? I'll have you know *you* were breast-fed. Look, if all you can do is mutter in your beard, why don't you go in the kitchen and make yourself useful? There's a bottle of champagne in the fridge which could do with opening.'

'Great!' Lewis said. 'Olivia is very fond of champagne.'

Olivia had no intention of going back to the office in a tipsy state. 'Sorry,' she apologised swiftly. 'The doctor told me alcohol was a no-no during the early months of pregnancy.'

'One little sip won't hurt, surely,' Betty said. 'We have to toast the baby properly.'

'One little sip, then. You can share the rest of the bottle with your mum,' Olivia added, giving Lewis a sweetly mocking smile in return. 'After all, *you're* not pregnant. I can always drive us back to the office.'

He scowled behind his mother's back. Betty smiled as she steered Olivia across the large living room and out onto a spacious balcony where a delicious spread awaited them.

'I can't tell you how glad I am to meet you at last, Olivia,' she said warmly as she pulled a chair out for everyone. 'Please be assured that you have my full support in your decision to have my son's child, and my full support in your decision not to marry him.'

Olivia blinked her surprise, and her confusion. She sat down at the table, her expression thoughtful. 'I...I'm not sure how to take that.'

Betty sat down opposite her before answering. 'Both of you have had recent serious relationships,' she elaborated. 'Lewis is still not legally extricated from marriage to a woman who damaged his faith and trust in the female sex. I gather you experienced a similar trauma at the hands of a young man you hoped to marry. It's never good to rush into another commitment until you're sure it will last, no matter how well suited you might seem to be on the surface.'

Olivia breathed a sigh of relief. 'I'm so glad you feel that way, Mrs Altman.'

'I do. But, knowing my son, he's going to do everything to pressure you into doing what he thinks he wants. And it seems he wants you to marry him. Which is why I have arranged to have the deeds of one of the apartments in this block transferred into your name. That way, you will be financially independent. And you'll have an excellent babysitter not far away,' she added with a wide warm smile.

Olivia could hardly believe what she was hearing. 'That's simply wonderful, Betty, but it...it's far too generous. I do have some money, you know. Some savings.'

'Which you should keep for a rainy day. Number three is currently vacant,' she rattled on. 'It's a ground-floor apartment with a nice little garden court-yard and its own clothesline. Nothing worse than cart-ing washing and prams up and down stairs and lifts. You'll like it, I'm sure.'

Olivia was feeling both touched and overwhelmed. 'Does…does Lewis know about this?'

'Not yet.'

'He's going to be angry with you.'

'He'll get over it.'

'What will I get over?'

Betty flashed her son a sweet smile while Olivia stiffened in her chair.

'I'm having one of the apartments in this building gifted over to Olivia.'

'What a good idea!' he exclaimed, and began pour-ing the champagne.

The women exchanged puzzled glances. Olivia found it extremely suspicious that Lewis was taking this news so well.

'You don't object?' she ventured.

'Why should I? It's better than you staying in that cockroach-infested dump you're living in at the mo-ment.'

'It is *not* cockroach infested!' she protested, though she had indeed spotted the odd nasty lurking in the kitchen cupboards. She'd driven the landlord mad with complaints last summer.

'*All* flats that old in Sydney have cockroaches,'

Lewis pronounced. 'So when are you moving in here?'

'I can't move till the lease runs out in another month.'

'No worries,' Betty said. 'The solicitor will have done all the paperwork by then. Meanwhile, Lewis can take you furniture shopping.'

'Can't do that, Mum. I'm not allowed to buy Olivia anything, am I?' He deposited a glass of champagne in front of each of them and sat down. 'Olivia has forbidden it.'

'Not even for the nursery?' Betty was aghast.

Olivia felt herself weakening. It *would* be lovely to have the sort of nursery for her baby that you saw in the furniture catalogues, with everything so new and fresh and pretty.

'Oh, all right,' she said. 'But only for the nursery, mind. I already have quite good furniture I can use in the other rooms.'

Lewis gave her a sharp look, but didn't persist with that subject. 'Let's raise our glasses in a toast,' he suggested. 'To my son or daughter. May he or she be healthy and happy.'

'To *our* son or daughter,' Olivia corrected him. 'May he or she be loved.'

Their eyes clashed while Betty chuckled. She raised her glass and clicked it against the other two, giving them both a drily amused glance. 'To my grandchild,' she finished firmly. 'May he or she have a will of iron. Otherwise, life with you two is going to be a three-ring circus!'

CHAPTER FIFTEEN

'WELL, how did it go?' Lila asked avidly once the two girls were alone in the ladies' room.

'So-so,' Olivia said.

Lewis had remained in a bright but slightly sardonic mood all through lunch, as though he knew he didn't stand a chance of winning any arguments against two women. He had, however, fallen broodingly silent on the drive back to the office. Olivia wasn't sure if he was angry with *her*, or his mother. He hadn't made a fuss about the flat business, but he hadn't been pleased, either. She'd seen it in his eyes a couple of times.

'Did he like the way you looked?' Lila queried while Olivia took off the red top and the shoes.

She hesitated. 'To be honest, I think he preferred me the way I was before.'

Lila's nose wrinkled. 'What's wrong with the man? Doesn't he have red blood running through his veins?'

'Not when he's at work, apparently.'

'How disappointing.'

'Oh, I don't know, Lila. I don't think it's a good idea to mix business with pleasure. Affairs between secretaries and their bosses are fraught with danger.'

'Oh, pooh! That's the sort of old-fashioned rubbish mothers tell you!'

Not mine, Olivia thought ruefully as she made her way slowly back to her office.

Lewis was sitting at her desk when she returned. He rose at the sight of her, one eyebrow arching at her prim white blouse and sensible shoes.

'It's no use, Olivia,' he drawled. 'The damage has been done.'

'Damage?'

'I can still see that red top in my mind's eye. The same red, I might add, which is still making your mouth look so sexy it's downright sinful. Frankly, I don't think you're keeping your part of the bargain by being provocative in the office. If I didn't know better, I'd think you *wanted* me to ravish you on my desk!'

Olivia's heart began thudding wildly. *Did* she?

'But I'm a man of my word,' he grated out. 'Which is why I'm going home early. I trust tomorrow will find you wearing nothing to raise my blood pressure. Or anything else in my body!'

Things didn't improve on Tuesday. Even with Olivia dressed drearily from head to toe and all vestiges of make-up removed, Lewis's temper remained short and the tension between them palpable. Her attempt to soften things by telling him about her visit to the doctor the previous night was an abject failure. He listened impatiently to her news that all was well and that she'd received a referral to a good obstetrician.

'How do you know he's good?' he snapped.

She threw him a helpless look.

'I'll have him checked out, as well as the hospital

he delivers in. I'm not having you going to some second-rate quack.'

She sighed and his eyes narrowed. 'Why are you sighing? Aren't you feeling well? Is there something I don't know about?'

'No. The doctor says I'm just fine. In fact, she said I'm in perfect health.'

'What about sex?'

'What about it?'

A muscle in his jaw contracted. 'Did you ask if that presented a problem?'

'Yes.'

'And?'

'No problem...provided...um—' She broke off and bit her bottom lip.

'Provided what?' he demanded irritably.

'Provided my partner isn't too rough.'

Lewis looked appalled. 'Is that what's been worrying you? You think I'm some sort of animal who can't control himself?'

'No!'

'Yeah, right,' he muttered, then fell sullenly silent.

'Lewis...'

His eyes snapped up, his expression tortured. 'What now?'

'Nothing,' she said, and fled.

By Wednesday morning, Olivia was a mess, torn by doubts and desire. It wasn't Lewis she was afraid of but her own weak self. She had hardly slept all night for thinking about him, and wanting him. Her need was a deep ache inside her. If his plan was to use sex to coerce her into marriage then he was onto a sure thing. She could hardly think straight any more.

He had told her the day before not to bother to come into the office. He would pick her up in a taxi around ten. It was already nine and still she wasn't packed or dressed.

Olivia dithered for ages, tempted to adopt a provocative image once more. Finally, pride prevailed and she stuck with one of her sensible black suits, her only concession to the desires running through her veins being a cream silk shirtmaker blouse which clung a little and showed her bust to advantage. Her hair she wore half up, secured on her crown with a tortoiseshell clasp, the rest left to hang in a glossy dark curtain halfway down her back.

No way could Lewis accuse her of being overly seductive. It was still, however, a subtly sexier look than her norm. On top of that, she packed a great little red and black silk dress in the latest petticoat style which didn't crush and *was* provocative. She'd bought it last November with Nicholas and Christmas parties in mind. Now, she had Lewis in mind. In mind and in body!

At two minutes to ten she shakily draped her jacket over her arm, picked up her case and handbag and went downstairs. She was waiting impatiently on the pavement with her overnight bag at her feet when the taxi pulled up at five past ten. When the driver popped out and picked up her case, she quickly climbed in beside Lewis in the back seat.

'Good morning,' she said.

'Morning,' he returned brusquely.

Their eyes ran over each other, with Olivia the first to look away. He looked so handsome and sexy in that dark blue suit. She didn't know how she was going to keep her mind on business today. She was already an emotional wreck, hopelessly on edge and physically aroused.

'The domestic or international terminal, mate?' the cab driver asked as he climbed back in.

'Domestic. Qantas.'

'Right.'

Olivia was grateful they weren't alone, even if it was only a cab driver preventing their conversation from becoming awkward. She leant back against the seat, sighing in an attempt to get a handle on her already quickening heartbeat.

'I hope that doesn't mean you're tired,' Lewis muttered under his breath.

Her head rolled sideways till their eyes met. 'I didn't sleep all that well last night,' she admitted softly.

His hard blue gaze melted, and, with it, her heart.

'Neither did I,' he admitted just as softly. 'But never mind,' he murmured, and his mouth curved into the most seductive smile. 'We will tonight.'

Tonight was an eternity coming.

The flight down. The drive from Tullarmarine into Melbourne. The long, boring afternoon, listening to two smooth-talking but essentially uninspiring advertising executives. By the time they caught the lift up to their hotel room around six, Olivia's tension had converted to two badly aching legs.

'You look tired,' Lewis said, frowning over at her.

'Nothing a relaxing bath won't cure.'

'After your bath, I think you should have a lie-down before dinner.'

She smiled, despite the constriction in her chest. 'Is that an order or an invitation?'

'A sensible suggestion. I don't like my dinner partners nodding off during the soup.'

'Maybe you should order room service.'

'Good thinking. That way it won't matter if you do nod off.'

'Can I still wear the sexy dress I brought with me?'

'You brought a sexy dress?'

'I thought I might need to seduce you again.'

He laughed. 'That's the funniest thing I've heard all year.'

'Do you want to make love before dinner, or after?'

'All three,' he said, and she frowned.

His smile was wry. 'Before. During. *And* after.'

His answer delighted her, and she laughed. 'I didn't realise you were that hungry.'

'Honey,' he murmured, and she quivered at the look in his eyes, 'you've no idea.'

He showed her just how hungry. Before. During. And very definitely after. Yet for all his insatiable passion he was so sweet and so gentle, Olivia was finally moved to tears.

When he saw them, Lewis was immediately alarmed.

'You're crying!' he cried, blue eyes pained and panicky. 'What is it, darling? Have I hurt you? Are you all right?'

'No, no, I'm fine.' She hastened to reassure him,

but the 'darling' had brought another rush of tears. Would she ever really be his darling? Dear God, she wanted to be, more than anything in the world. 'I...I'm just a bit emotional at the moment,' she choked out. 'You know how it is.'

He cupped her face and frowned down into her swimming eyes. 'I can *see* how it is,' he murmured, 'and it bothers me terribly. I hate seeing you cry, Olivia. I hate to think you're unhappy about having my baby.'

'But I'm not, Lewis,' she denied. 'Truly. I—'

'You'd rather the father was someone else,' he broke in bleakly.

'No. Never! I think you're going to make a wonderful father.'

His eyes cleared and a happy light glowed within their beautiful blue depths. 'You do?'

'Oh, yes. I'm going to be so proud to introduce you as my baby's father.'

'Proud,' he repeated thoughtfully.

'Yes. Now go to sleep, Lewis. You must be awfully tired.'

His smile was soft and wry. 'Am I being told that's enough for tonight?'

'Yes.'

'Don't forget who's the boss here.'

'I haven't,' she said, smiling wryly back. 'At the moment, in this bed, it's me.'

'Is that so?'

Olivia knew immediately she shouldn't have challenged him. It was like waving a red rag at a bull. 'Want to put money on that?' he drawled.

'No.'

'Why?'

'I'd probably lose.'

'Do I detect a lack of faith in your maintaining the upper hand here?'

'My form where you're concerned hasn't been too good so far.'

'Meaning?'

'Meaning I seem to be putty in your hands, boss.'

'God, I like the sound of that. Shall we put it to the test once more?'

Her heart turned over then started to race. 'You're the boss.'

They flew back from Melbourne on Thursday evening, Lewis in a jubilant mood. Not only had he proved himself *el supremo* in bed the previous night, but the last of the three advertising agencies they'd visited had proved a winner, with the trio of female partners coming up with a presentation which found favour with both the owner of Altman Industries and his personal assistant.

Olivia thought their idea was brilliant and had said so openly. To make ads featuring a range of nice-looking but ordinary women who held ordinary jobs and lived full but ordinary lives was both appealing and good business. The ads would concentrate on four married women with children, juggling work, house and family. The advertising agency had suggested a variety of careers from a supermarket cashier to a kindergarten teacher to a car mechanic to a community nurse. The ads would follow these women through their day, subtly slipping in when and where they used their All Woman products and ending with a tag line about their being All Women! It was a simple concept, but simplicity often succeeded.

'Come home with me,' Lewis said abruptly as they waited for a taxi at Mascot airport.

Olivia had been afraid this would happen. She'd surrendered to Lewis far too much the previous night. He probably thought she'd do anything he wanted now, including marry him, when he next asked.

And he was probably right.

But that didn't mean she was going to let him think she was easy.

'I'd like to, Lewis,' she said with a sweetly apologetic smile. 'I really would. But I'm tired. And I don't have any more fresh clothes with me.'

'I have a well equipped laundry with a dryer,' he told her silkily, and reached out to take her hand in his, lifting it to his mouth.

'Please don't, Lewis,' she said, and snatched her hand away. 'You're embarrassing me.'

He stared at her, a frown of black frustration gathering on his face. 'I thought, after last night, we'd moved on from playing games. I thought you wanted me as much as I wanted you.'

Olivia glanced around, aware of the queue of people in front and behind them. 'Lewis, this is not the time or the place,' she said stiffly.

'If you don't come home with me now…tonight, Olivia,' he grated out, 'I won't ask you again. I can promise you that.'

Olivia could not believe he would stoop to blackmail to get her into bed with him on command.

'I didn't realise you could be such a jerk,' she said angrily.

He glared at her, then turned away, his expression hard and dismissive. She recognised the look. It was one he adopted before firing an employee.

Despair twisted deep inside Olivia. So much for the depth of his caring about her. Turn him down once, and that was the end of her. She felt like crying. But she didn't. She stood beside the man she loved and let her heart break in silence.

CHAPTER SIXTEEN

FRIDAY morning found Olivia feeling unwell. It wasn't morning sickness, but a deep melancholy of spirit. She had to drag herself out of bed. Breakfast was a chore. Showering and dressing almost impossible.

The girls behind Reception stared at her when she arrived for work twenty minutes late. She mumbled some lame excuse and hurried down the corridor, only to meet Lewis halfway along.

His face mirrored abject apology at the sight of her, but she was not in the mood to forgive him. A deep depression had taken possession of her heart overnight, plus a deep resentment. She was hard pushed even to say good morning in a civil tone.

His hand shot out to grab her arm when she went to push past him. 'Olivia, please... I'm sorry... I didn't mean it.'

When she refused to look at him, he sighed and let her go.

'Won't you at least accept my apology?' he asked softly.

She stiffened and still did not look at him. 'No,' she bit out. 'Now I really should get to my desk. I'm late.'

'Olivia, I...'

Her head snapped round and she set cold eyes upon

him. 'If you think I'm going to discuss our private relationship in public again, then you can think again, Lewis Altman. Not that we *have* a private relationship any more!'

She left him without another word or a backward glance, marching down the corridor towards her office. Tossing her bag on the floor beside her desk, she sat down and got to work. Or pretended to get to work. How could she possibly concentrate with her heart pounding and her head whirling?

Ten minutes later, Lewis returned from wherever it was he'd gone to and stood stubbornly in front of her desk. 'We have to talk about this, Olivia.'

She didn't even look up. 'Not now, Lewis.'

'Yes, *now*!' he roared.

Her own temper flared and her eyes flew up to his. 'We have nothing further to discuss,' she said with cold fury. 'You are not the man I thought you were. You're arrogant and selfish and self-centred. You will have my resignation on your desk within the hour.'

Disbelief and horror were stamped on his face. 'But you can't! I mean...for pity's sake, Olivia, you're having my baby!'

'Which is all you care about, isn't it?' she threw at him. 'That's all women are good for to you. Having babies. Other than sex, of course. Or being your secretary. I sympathise with Dinah now. If I was unfortunate enough to be married to you, I'd be divorcing you too, baby or no baby. You know nothing of a woman's needs. You know nothing of love. Your vocabulary begins and ends with what Lewis Altman *wants*.'

Olivia could see that her words were finding their mark; Lewis was looking both stricken and guilty. But she hadn't finished yet. She'd spent all night thinking about things and she wanted her say.

'You know, I once believed that underneath your focused drive and ambition you were basically a good and generous man. And you *can* be, but only when being good and generous gets you what you want,' she added sneeringly. 'Which of course, at the moment, is your precious baby. I said you'd make a good father but I doubt that too now. Will your child be a real person to you, or just another product you've created, a reflection of your enormous ego? I made the mistake of calling you deep once. You're not deep. You're so shallow, it's unbelievable. Now I suggest you leave me alone for the rest of the day, Lewis, or I'll get up and walk out of here right now. I don't *need* you, you know. I don't need this job and I certainly don't need your money. I'll manage just fine by myself.'

For a moment, she was sure he was going to argue with her. His mouth actually opened. But he closed it again, his eyes strangely unreadable.

Turning, he walked slowly into his office and closed the door behind him with suspicious softness.

The moment she was alone, Olivia's chin began to wobble. She knew she'd gone too far. He wasn't that bad, really. It had been her hurt talking. And her temper. Now she'd alienated him entirely. She didn't really want to resign. What ever had possessed her to say so?

Oh, Olivia, Olivia, you stupid, stupid girl!

She was sitting there contemplating going into
Lewis's office with her tail between her legs and an
apology on her lips, when the door of *her* office
opened and there stood Nicholas, smiling.

'Hi there, Liv,' he said, and searched her face for
a possible reaction.

When Olivia made no reply he closed the door behind him and turned back to face her. 'I dropped over
to the flat to see you Wednesday night,' he explained
as he crossed the room. 'But you weren't in. Then
yesterday I rang here, and was told you were in
Melbourne with the boss on business and wouldn't be
back till today. I hope you don't mind my coming
here, but I just couldn't wait till tonight.'

Olivia could only shake her head, amazed both at
Nicholas's showing up, plus her own reaction to his
reappearance in her life. Not to mention his appearance.

There'd been a time when she'd thought him drop-
dead gorgeous, with his boyish blond looks and tall,
slender frame. Now, as she stared up at him, all she
could see was the boy in his unformed face and body,
both of which were on the soft side. Even the trendy
new suit he was wearing didn't mask his immaturity.
If anything, it made him look younger.

Her taste in men had matured, it seemed. She now
preferred the tall, dark and sophisticated variety, ones
who had experienced eyes, hard muscles and even
harder mouths.

Ah, Lewis, she thought momentarily, her heart contracting.

It was a relief, though, to see her ex in the flesh,

because she realised once and for all just how 'ex' he was, in her mind and her heart. If nothing else, seeing Nicholas again had achieved that.

'What is it you want, Nicholas?' she asked, her tone betraying nothing but puzzlement.

'*You*, Olivia,' he said, and she laughed. She couldn't help it.

His expression was pained. 'I know I've hurt you, and I'm sorry,' he said with a soulful look on his weakly pretty face. 'My only excuse is that I was young. And stupid.'

'You still *are*, Nicholas.'

'Not any more,' he insisted, and hurried around to drop onto his knees beside her desk. Olivia cried out when he grabbed her hands and crushed them to his chest. 'It wasn't till I left you that I realised how much I loved you,' he insisted passionately. 'I can't live without you. I need you. Please let me come back. I promise never to look at another woman again. I don't know why I did in the first place. Yvette was a right slut. Not like you. You're the best. I know that now. We'll get married as soon as you want. Say you forgive me, Liv, darling. Tell me you still love me. God, I don't know what I'm going to do if you don't.'

'You're going to get the hell out of here!'

Olivia gasped at the sound of Lewis's voice, snatching her hands away from Nicholas's grasp and whirling in her chair to face the furious-faced father of her child. He was standing a few feet away from her desk and looking down at Nicholas as though he would like to kill him. 'Olivia isn't taking you back, you snivelling, lily-livered bastard. I'll have you know that she—'

'Lewis!' she broke in before he could blurt out the news of her pregnancy. 'Please don't,' she pleaded, frowning her distress.

'You *can't* be thinking of going back to him,' Lewis said, obviously shaken by the thought.

'I'm not,' she said, and wished that Lewis's passion was for her, and not their baby.

But she knew differently.

Nicholas had risen to his feet. His face had gone red and he was looking very confused. 'You don't mean that, Liv. You and I were meant to be together. You always said so.'

'I'm sorry, Nicholas,' she reiterated more firmly. 'You're too late. I don't want you any more.'

'I don't believe you!'

'You heard what the lady said,' Lewis snapped. 'She doesn't want you any more. Now get lost!'

Nicholas swung round to face Lewis. 'Listen, *mate*, nobody asked you. Why don't you just butt out? You might be Olivia's boss but I happen to be her boyfriend. She's *my* bird. Always was and always will be!'

'Is that so?' Lewis marched around the desk, while a suddenly fearful Nicholas staggered back a step or two. 'Now *you* listen, *mate*!' Lewis ground out, jabbing a furious forefinger into his chest. 'Olivia might have been your bird once. But she's *my* bird now. Yes, you heard me, she's mine. For now and always. I love her and need her more than you ever did. And I believe she loves and needs me back.'

'Loves *you*?' Nicholas sneered. 'Liv doesn't love *you*!'

'Yes, I do, Nicholas,' she confessed, standing up and turning blurred eyes to Lewis. 'I *do* love him. I've loved him for ages...'

Olivia watched Lewis's eyes open wide with surprise before they softened and filled with such charged emotion, she could hardly bear it. He loved her. He really loved her.

'But...but...' Nicholas was blustering.

'Not only do I love him,' she went on, her melting gaze all for Lewis, 'but I'm having his baby.'

'Having his *baby*!' Nicholas squawked. 'When did this happen? I've only been gone two bloody months. Geez, you were having it off with him before I left you, weren't you? All this time, I've been feeling guilty about Yvette and you and the boss here were already at it like rabbits! And I thought you were something special. Hell, you're nothing but a slut like the rest of them.'

It all happened so quickly. One minute, Nicholas was standing there. The next, Lewis had him by the scruff of the neck and was dragging him down the corridor where he literally threw him through the— thankfully—open side door. He looked very satisfied with himself as he stalked back, brushing off his hands, oblivious of the people who'd popped out of their offices behind him to see what was going on.

Oblivious, too, was Olivia as she ran through her office door to throw herself into his arms. 'Oh, Lewis,' she cried.

He cupped her face and looked seriously into her

eyes. 'You did mean it, didn't you? About loving me?'

'Of course I meant it.'

'For *ages*?' His voice was disbelieving.

'I knew my feelings had changed the day I came back to work this year. But I was really sure the morning Dinah showed up. I was so torn up by jealousy, I knew it had to be love.'

'Jealousy will do it every time,' he said, nodding. 'When I saw Nicholas kneeling in front of you, holding your hands, I wanted to tear him limb from limb. When I heard him ask you to go back to him, I wanted to scream out *no* so loudly that they'd have heard me across at Bondi. I was afraid, you see, that you still loved him.'

'I haven't loved him for a long time. It's you I love.'

'Tell me again, my darling. It's music to my ears.'

'I love you, Lewis.'

'And I love you. God, how I love you!'

The spontaneous applause behind them had the pair whirling and blushing. At least, Olivia was blushing. Lewis simply looked smug.

'While we have an audience, darling, I'm going to ask you again. Will you marry me?'

Olivia could feel fresh tears pricking. But this was not the moment for a faint heart. 'Yes,' she said, loud and clear. 'Yes, I will.'

'Aah,' was all Lewis said, and gathered her to him.

CHAPTER SEVENTEEN

'YOU'RE so beautiful,' Lewis crooned to his newborn son who was lying in his father's arms looking up at him with wide, alert eyes.

'The nurse said he's too beautiful for a boy,' Olivia said from her bed. She was finally feeling almost human, the memory of that last horrific hour before the birth fading a little.

Next time, she vowed, she was going to get to the hospital early enough to have all of those lovely pain-killers she'd planned on having. Unfortunately, she'd been tricked into a false sense of security by the mildness of her early labour and stayed home far too long. Once her waters broke, however, everything had escalated very quickly, and what was bearable had swiftly moved up several notches to unbearable. The drive to the hospital had seemed appallingly long, yet in fact had only been a fifteen-minute trip in the dead of night. Still, by the time they'd arrived and she'd been shown to the maternity section, Olivia had been on the verge of screaming. When the doctor had told her it was too late for an epidural, or anything else for that matter, she *had* groaned her agony, and kept on groaning till her son arrived forty minutes later.

'He's going to be a lady-killer all right,' Lewis said, smiling proudly down at the wee infant again. 'Especially with those eyes of his. They're *your* eyes, darling,' he added, coming over to plant a soft kiss on Olivia's forehead.

'But my eyes aren't blue,' she pointed out.

'Silly-billy,' Lewis said gently. 'All babies are born with blue eyes. But his are darker than mine even now. Give him a few months and he'll have his mother's beautiful big brown eyes.'

Olivia flushed with pleasure at the compliment. Lewis was always saying sweet things to her, making her feel so very special. There wasn't anything about her he didn't like, not even her passion for making lists and planning every single detail in advance.

Life, however, had a way of upsetting her plans every now and then, such as the way she would act during her labour. She'd been going to be so serene, not groaning and thrashing around.

'We'd better finalise his name before everyone descends upon us, Olivia,' Lewis said. 'You know what it'll be like. They'll start making suggestions. Best we head them off at the pass with a good solid name, one which can't be shortened or changed to something obnoxious. I'll never forget being called Lew at school. Sounded like a toilet.'

Olivia laughed. 'In that case I guess Lew junior is out?'

'Heaven forbid.'

'You choose all our boys' names, Lewis,' she said, sensing he had something in mind. 'I'll choose the girls'.' She'd already made a long list of girls' names after her mother had told her she was carrying a girl for sure, because she was carrying so low. So much for old wives' tales! Next time, she'd just ask the doctor what the sex was when she had the ultrasound. Olivia preferred being prepared in advance.

'I think I'd like to call him Christopher,' Lewis said. 'He'll get Chris, of course. But I quite like that, don't you?'

'Very much. But what about a second name? Do you think we might use Dad's name?'

'Christopher David Altman,' Lewis said slowly, and beamed. 'That certainly has a ring to it, doesn't it?'

'Strong,' Olivia agreed. 'Like his father.'

Lewis looked at her, his eyes full of love and pride. 'Not as strong as his mother. I couldn't have borne what you did today, darling. Yet you're already talking about having more children. I am in awe of your strength, and your courage.'

'Don't deceive yourself, Lewis, I'm not that brave. Neither am I a masochist! Next time, I'm going to be parked on this hospital doorstep at the very first twinge. Then I'm going to have every pain-killer known to mankind!'

Lewis nodded in agreement. 'Do you think I could have a few at the same time? It's not the easiest thing in the world, you know, watching and worrying about your beloved. You feel so helpless.'

Olivia's heart turned over at the word 'beloved'. 'You weren't helpless, my darling husband. You were a tower of strength.'

'But all I could do was hold your hand!'

'But you held it very well.'

He laughed, then bent to kiss her again. 'This is the happiest day of my life.'

'Mine too.'

'I'll have to set to work finding a house for us to live in. We can't stay in that unit for ever.'

When Lewis's house had been auctioned several months back, he'd moved with Olivia into the unit his mother had given her.

'It's perfectly fine for the time being, Lewis. Just think. We have a wonderful built-in babysitter with your mother upstairs. She's been dying to get her hands on the baby ever since she found out I was expecting.'

'True. Er…do you think you'll ever want to go back to work, Olivia?'

Olivia was surprised by the question. She'd categorically told Lewis months before that she didn't want to work after the baby was born. Maybe she'd sent a mixed message by going into the office every day till the birth, but that had been because she would have been more nervous awaiting the birth alone at home. It hadn't been till two weeks back, when she'd been approaching her due date, that she'd finally organised a replacement secretary for Lewis.

Not one to leave anything to chance, Olivia had used an employment agency who'd followed her instructions to a T and sent along a ruthlessly efficient woman in her early fifties who was a career spinster and the furthest thing from a glamour-puss you could find. Olivia would never feel insecure with Barbara Hoskins at the helm.

Not that she thought Lewis would ever be tempted to betray her. She just didn't want to create any stress for him in his working life. 'Certainly not in the foreseeable future, darling,' she reassured Lewis. 'It's going to take me the next eight years to complete our family of four. Then another five before the youngest goes to school. That makes thirteen years all up.'

'My God, do you realise I'll be nearly fifty by then?'

'And I'll have turned forty!' she wailed.

'Ah, but you'll still be all woman, my love. Which reminds me, I received the sales results yesterday for the first quarter since the All Woman launch.'

'And?'

'They leave the figures for the All Man products for dead. We can hardly keep up with the orders. Those ads have been a great success.'

'Oh, Lewis, that's marvellous.'

'Yes. But not as marvellous as this,' he said as he laid his beautiful and now sleeping baby boy in his crib. 'This is something else, isn't it?'

'It certainly is,' Olivia murmured, battling to control the wave of emotion which was flowing through her.

Lewis looked up, and she could see he was just as moved. 'I love you, Olivia Altman,' he choked out.

'I love you too,' she returned softly.

He was kissing her when his head suddenly snapped up. 'I can hear people coming down the corridor.'

'It'll be my parents,' Olivia said.

'And my mother. Wake up, son, you have visitors,' he said, and scooped the baby back up into his arms.

Olivia thought she had never seen a man so proud or so happy as he displayed his son to the oohs and aahs of the various grandparents. After a few minutes of admiring her grandson, Olivia's mother slipped away to give her daughter a big hug.

'Congratulations,' she said quietly. 'I'm so happy for you. He's so beautiful. And that was a lovely thought, naming him after Dave.'

Olivia smiled at her mother who was looking ten years younger these days. So was her dad, for that matter. 'I'm very lucky,' she said.

'Luck has nothing to do with it, Olivia. I knew as soon as you told me about Lewis that he was the man for you.'

Olivia laughed. 'You did, didn't you?'

'I was telling Betty as much just a few minutes ago. She felt the same about you as soon as she met you. She said she knew straight away that Lewis had met his perfect match at long last!'

Olivia had to agree. They *were* a perfect match, she and Lewis. They wanted the same things in life and felt the same way about so much. But, most important of all, they felt the same way about each other.

As though reading her mind, he glanced over his shoulder at her, smiling a smile full of such love that her heart filled to overflowing. Her mother might not think luck had anything to do with it, but she felt very lucky indeed. A handsome and loving husband. A beautiful and healthy son. Not to mention a supportive and caring family.

Money was all very well, but it didn't buy happiness. No, she would never get so carried away with material things and so-called security that she would lose sight of what really mattered.

Love and family were the keys to happiness, Olivia decided as she smiled back at her husband.

Love...and family.

HARLEQUIN PRESENTS®

Passion™

Looking for stories that **sizzle?**

Wanting a read that has
a little extra **spice?**

Harlequin Presents® is thrilled to bring
you romances that turn up the **heat!**

In November 1999 there's *The Revenge Affair*
by Susan Napier, Harlequin Presents® #2062

Every other month there'll be a
PRESENTS PASSION book by one of your
favorite authors.

And in January 2000 look out for
One Night with his Wife **by Lynne Graham,**
Harlequin Presents® #2073

*Pick up a PRESENTS PASSION—
where seduction is guaranteed!*

Available wherever Harlequin books are sold.

HARLEQUIN®
Makes any time special ™